BRIDES AND BLADES

BAKERS AND BULLDOG MYSTERIES

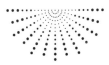

ROSIE SAMS

SWEETBOOKHUB.COM

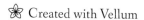

BAKERS AND BULLDOGS COZY MYSTERIES

Dear reader,

It is such an honor to share this book with you. I have always been a fan of three things, my French bulldog, baking, and sweet cozy mysteries.

What could be better than curling up with a dog on your lap, with a nice cake at your side, and with a cozy mystery to read?

I have recently joined a team of sweet authors at SweetBookHub.com

Our aim is to entertain you with sweet books that you will love to read.

I am so pleased that they have given me the chance

to share my books with you. Join our Exclusive Reader Club to find out more, it's free to join.

This is my second book, you can grab the first one Strawberries and Sweet Lies here.

Love and kisses,

Rosie Sams

CHAPTER ONE

$\mathcal{M}$elody Marshall's nose scrunched in concentration as she tried for the dozenth time to choose between red roses or blue chrysanthemums. As a skilled baker and decorator, she generally had a rather easy time deciding on color-schemes and adornment selections. However, this time, the desire for the cake to be perfect had her second-guessing every flower combination she tried.

"You're overthinking this, Melody," she told herself, stepping back to survey the dummy cake. "Aren't I, Smudge?"

Melody looked over to where her French Bulldog spent the bulk of her time to find her lying flat on her back, snoring softly.

"Well, you're no help," she remarked with a chuckle, turning back to the task at hand.

Melody set aside the red roses, gathering up a few chrysanthemums once again. She tentatively placed them across the cake, spacing them perfectly along the top tier that would be chocolate draped with white frosting on the real cake. Taking a few steps back, she took in her work. She was quick to shake her head. Beautiful as the vibrant blue flowers were, they still didn't feel right, not at all.

"Too much like a coming-out ball... she's a bride, not a debutante, for goodness sakes," she muttered to herself as she stepped back toward the cake and quickly removed the offending flowers.

She replaced them with the roses. Yes, the red flowers suited Dorinda Mitchum (soon to be Dorinda Werther), much better. The blue was far too juvenile.

Melody breathed a sigh of relief at finally having made a decision. Nothing but the best would do for the daughter of Port Warren's doctor, Dr. Ambrose Mitchum, and Melody wanted the cake to be absolutely perfect as each and every other aspect of the wedding was sure to be."

"There," Melody said once she'd completed the top layer.

A contented sigh escaped from the sleeping Smudge, drawing Melody's eyes in the pup's direction. The Frenchie lay sprawled on her back, grey and white paws up in the air, her eyes tightly closed and her mouth hanging open. Her pink tongue crept out of her mouth as she continued to snore with abandon.

"You're so lucky, Smudge," Melody said, chuckling. "You don't have to worry about any of this wedding stuff."

Melody turned back to the cake, intent on completing the whole design right then since she finally had the color scheme figured out. However, the sound of raised voices from the kitchen drew her attention towards the door, and she frowned. Smudge, startled out of her tranquil state, leaped up and rushed in the direction of the commotion.

Melody exhaled, reluctantly setting aside her decorating tools, more than a little displeased at the idea of abandoning her project after inspiration had finally struck. However, as the voices of her two assistants continued to rise, it was made abundantly clear that she had little choice.

Melody walked swiftly from her office, followed by Smudge, who trotted dutifully toward the scene. The pair arrived in the kitchen to find Melody's two employees huddled over a large stainless mixing bowl.

"That's not how you fold ingredients, Leslie," Kerry said. Her tall frame was taut with vehemence as she towered over her coworker, her flushed cheeks turning the color of the auburn hair escaping from her hairnet. "These macaroons are going to be flat, thanks to you!"

"Would you mind your own business?" Leslie retorted, angling away from Kerry, her arms wrapped protectively around the mixing bowl. "I've made many batches of macaroons in my life, and I will have you know that I've never had a batch go flat."

Though she hated breaking up cat-fights, Melody knew that it was time to step in. "Ladies, do we have a problem?"

Kerry turned toward Melody, her brows rising, arms crossed.

"Melody, if you want Dorinda's cake to be even close to acceptable, I wouldn't let Leslie within a mile of the kitchen when it comes time to bake for the wedding if I were you."

Leslie's mouth popped open in fury as she cradled the mixing bowl against her. It looked huge in front of her small frame. She nearly dropped the load of unbaked macaroon mix as she shoved her wire-rimmed glasses up on her nose, glaring at Kerry in rage.

"You have some nerve! You never complained about my folding technique before today, and you know it. You've been hovering all day. Why don't you just mind your own business? This task doesn't take two of us, so why don't you stop micromanaging?"

"She's quite right, Kerry," Melody said. "There is a great deal to do, so I would appreciate it if you'd get started on bread for tomorrow." It was plain to see that that the stress of the wedding was getting to everyone, not only Melody, causing her employees to be even more irritated with each other than usual.

The best solution always seemed to be placing the two women in separate rooms in order to avoid further bickering—besides, keeping them quiet would allow her to finish the cake, which was her main goal.

"We have a lot to do," Melody went on. "I would also really appreciate it if you two work quietly on your *separate* tasks so I can focus on Dorinda's cake. If I don't get this cake right, the entire reputation we've built for this bakery will be in danger. Do you want all of our hard work to go right down the drain?"

Kerry and Leslie shook their heads wordlessly, looking very much like guilty school kids. If she hadn't been so stressed, Melody would have laughed at their comically child-like expressions.

"You both know how important this is. We've been entrusted with a monumental task, and I need to be able to count on you two to help make it a success. I think I've had an epiphany about the color-scheme, so if you two will just hold down the fort while I finish up, you would be fulfilling my greatest wish. Can I count on you for that?"

Kerry tucked the auburn hair desperately trying to

escape completely from her hairnet aside, her expression solemn. "I'm sorry, Mel. I'll try to be more tolerant.

"Okay, good," Melody said with a sigh of relief. "Now," she went on, raising her arms much like a commanding officer. "To your work stations. Go."

Melody shook her head, thinking not for the first time that no other boss would put up with such squabbling from her workers. Still, both Kerry and Leslie had been with her since she first opened, and when push came to shove, they were like family. They'd made it through stressful situations at the bakery before, and they would do it again.

Though she was doubtful that the restored tranquility would last, Melody made a mad dash for her office, intent on being productive during the quiet she was afforded. However, fate had other plans, and the bell at the front door rang before she could retreat to her office, and the looming task of the dummy cake.

Two women entered the shop. Melody stopped short at the sight of Dorinda, the bride-to-be herself. She didn't recognize her companion, a young woman with a brunette bob, and a keen interest in the eclair section of the display case, which she immediately began studying with rapt attention. Dorinda and her friend chatted together as they drew near the glass display case to study the wide variety of decadent pastries.

Melody told herself that she was being ridiculous, lurking in the shadows, hiding from customers in her own shop. However, the fact that she desperately wished she'd made more progress on the cake before the bride's arrival made her wish to trot right back to her office and tell Kerry or Leslie to help Dorinda.

You'll have to talk with her about the cake sometime, so it might as well be now, Melody reminded herself. *Besides, you've made dozens of wedding cakes in your lifetime. This one is no different.*

Pep-talk completed, Melody pasted on a professional smile in an attempt to hide her nerves and stepped forward. "Well, good afternoon, Dorinda."

Dorinda looked up, tossing a lock of her salon-perfect strawberry blond hair over her shoulder as she straightened. Her blue eyes, already alight with the bride-to-be glow, were set off even further by the heavy make-up surrounding them along with the dark red lipstick coating her mouth.

"Hello, Melody. How are you?"

"Doing just fine. Is there something I can help you with?"

"We might get a few things from the case," Dorinda said with a slight laugh as her friend continued to peruse the sweets. "This is my maid of honor, Laurel."

Laurel turned her attention from the baked goods display at the sound of her name and offered Melody a nod. "Hello. I suppose you're the one whipping up Dorinda's wedding cake?"

Melody forced an enthusiastic note into her voice. "Yes, I certainly am. In fact, your timing is perfect."

My, you are good at pretending, Melody Marshall.

"I'm working on my decorating plans now. I would love for you to take a look so I can make sure you like where it's going."

Dorinda's eyes lit up at the prospect. "I have to admit that is just what I was hoping for. We just came from the make-up artist who is contracted for the wedding and had such a great time." She clapped her hands together and chirped, "Wasn't it fun, Laurel?"

Laurel only nodded, and Melody wondered at her less-than-convincing reaction.

"Well, right this way," she said, starting down the hallway with Smudge and the two women on her heels. Melody led the way into the room, turning just in time to see the future bride's reaction to her first sight of the half-completed dummy cake.

"Oh, it's beautiful! The colors are marvelous!" Dorinda exclaimed, moving in to take a closer look.

Though she came from a highly influential family, Dorinda was just another excited bride like so many Melody had worked with before. She had nearly convinced herself that her previous fears had all been a waste of time when she caught the lackadaisical expression on the maid of honor's face.

"I love the flowers, Melody!" Dorinda continued to gush.

"I'm so happy to hear that," Melody smiled, relieved.

Dorinda turned then to Laurel, her face still aglow. "Laurie, what do you think?"

Before Laurel gave her opinion, Melody announced, "I have some samples of the almond cake we decided on using if you'd like to try it."

"Sure, I would love that!" Dorinda said.

"If you'll just follow me back up to the front." Melody and Smudge led the women back down the hallway. The women seated themselves at one of the small round tables situated by the window while Melody acquired the cupcakes from the case.

"You want to try one, don't you, Laurie?" Melody heard Dorinda ask her maid of honor as she neared the table.

Laurel shrugged. "Sure."

Laurel's lack of enthusiasm gave Melody pause. It seemed very strange considering she was supposed to be the bride's best friend. Melody had never been a maid of honor before but, weren't they supposed to be a tad more cheerful and overly enthusiastic about every little thing concerning the wedding? "All right, here you go, ladies," Melody said, distributing forks and cupcakes.

"Is there a restroom I can use?" Laurel asked, ignoring the cupcake and fork completely.

"Oh, sure. Just walk straight down the hallway where we just were, past the kitchen, and it will be on your right." Melody had to admit she was glad to see the maid of honor go so that she could focus on Dorinda, who eagerly tucked into her cupcake.

"Mmmmm," Dorinda hummed after the first bite. "It's delicious! I love the almond taste, and the frosting is perfect. Just the right amount of everything, just like the decorations!"

"I used Swiss meringue buttercream," Melody explained. "Not only is it less sweet than other frostings, but it withstands the heat beautifully, which makes it ideal for wedding cakes. We wouldn't want any of the edible flowers melting."

"No, we wouldn't!" Dorinda agreed, licking the frosting from her spoon. She shut her eyes for a minute, savoring the taste. "Wow, you really know how to do these things. I just know this cake is going to be a huge hit."

"I do hope so," Melody said. "But, in all truth, knowing that you are pleased is what matters most to me."

Dorinda smiled, taking another bite of cupcake. "I want everything to be just perfect," she said, her expression turning dreamy. "And you're making that possible, Melody."

"Being a bride suits you, Dorinda," Melody remarked. "You're positively glowing."

"I've never been so happy before in my entire life." Dorinda rested her chin in one hand, smiling absently. "I remember the day I met Robin like it was yesterday."

"How did you two meet? I haven't heard the story."

Dorinda chuckled, her expression a bit sheepish. "It sounds kind of silly, really," she said. "We were both in "The Night Owl." You know, the 24-hour coffee shop? Well, I was working on some work for the travel agency that my boss needed by the next day. I took computer classes in college where I learned how to use Word, Excel, and such, but I was having a terrible time with WordPress." She shook her head at the memory. "How web developers deal with all of that website stuff, I don't know. But I couldn't, for the life of me, figure it out and was getting so frustrated! It was nearly two o'clock in the morning, and I wasn't even halfway done. I was so worn out and tired from trying to figure it out that I started to cry. I was the only one there, so I figured it wouldn't bother anyone, and I just couldn't help myself.

"I was still crying into my coffee cup when I heard Robin approach my table and clear his throat. I tried to dry my eyes, but he had already noticed I was crying and asked if I was all right. Of course, I said I was fine, and he didn't believe me. He asked what I was doing out so late, and I said that I was trying to get some work done. That's when he told me that he had a case of insomnia and had decided to work on some patient charts instead of just lying awake. He asked me if there was anything he could help me with, and I told him about my WordPress troubles. Turns out he's a genius with that kind of thing and was able to fix what I'd been fiddling with for hours in a matter of minutes! He really is a genius with everything...."

"Sounds like a fairytale," Melody chuckled.

Melody laughed. "Yes, he did rescue me. And when

I think about the fact that in a few days... I'll marry the man I love. The one I want to spend the rest of my life with, I can hardly believe it's true."

"Well, you both have my very best wishes," Melody said.

Dorinda's smile stretched from ear to ear. "Thank you. And thank you for my cake. I'm so excited to see it when it's finished."

Just then, Laurel arrived back, showing no interest in her untouched cupcake. "Are you ready to get going, Dorinda?" she immediately asked.

Apparently taken aback, Dorinda blinked, glancing at Melody and then back at Laurel. For a moment, a frown creased her brow, but she seemed to brush off Laurel's strange attitude. "Oh, yeah, sure, we can go."

Once again, Melody was astounded at the maid of honor's lack of interest in the wedding preparations. She wondered what their relationship was like because, in her experience, best friends shared in each other's happiness. The disappointment on Dorinda's face made her feel exceedingly sorry for the bride-to-be.

Dorinda, however, pushed through Laurel's rudeness and stood with a smile. "I suppose that's it then. I would love to take a whole box full of pastries to go, but I'm afraid that wouldn't do me much good when it comes to fitting into my dress."

The woman's contagious, airy giggle made Melody laugh. "I'm sure you're right. After the wedding, perhaps."

Dorinda assured her she'd most certainly indulge after the wedding, thanked her again, and left along with a very silent and distant Laurel.

As Melody gathered up the forks and cupcake liners, thoughts of Dorinda and Laurel's visit continued to linger in her mind. It had been the strangest wedding cake consultation she'd ever had to date, that was for sure. Still, she couldn't quite put her finger on what had made it so odd. Perhaps Laurel's lack of interest was just a part of her personality....?

"Hey, Melody," Leslie said, wiping her hands with a dishtowel as she entered the front room.

Melody glanced up from wiping down the table, brows raised, dubiously. "Don't tell me you're coming to get me because you need a referee again."

Leslie waved off her boss' words. "Relax, Kerry and I are getting along just fine."

"Glad to hear it." After what had just transpired, Melody was most certainly not in the mood to break up another argument.

"How did the consultation go? Does Dorinda like the cake?"

"She seemed as pleased with it as any bride I've ever met," Melody said. She paused from cleaning the table, thinking. "There was something so strange about her maid of honor, though."

Leslie's brow furrowed. "What do you mean, strange?"

Melody shook her head. "She just wasn't excited about anything. Not the decorations, not the cake-tasting... It seems very odd."

"That is weird," Leslie agreed, grabbing a snickerdoodle from the display case. "It seems like the maid of honor is always the crazy one," she remarked around a mouthful of cookie. "You know, the one who is always going ballistic at the bachelorette party and making a big deal about every detail being perfect and stuff."

Melody released a wry chuckle. "My thoughts exactly. I can't ever imagine Laurel fulfilling that role. She just seemed so...cool. Way too unbothered."

"You can't imagine who fulfilling what role?" Kerry asked as she walked into the room.

"We're talking about Dorinda's maid of honor," Melody filled her in. "She doesn't seem very excited about the wedding."

Kerry's brows rose as she scanned the display case, taking down inventory on a notepad. "It's not as if her bridegroom is a particularly lively one either."

"Why do you say that?" Melody asked as she made her way behind the counter. Working on Dorinda's cake and then watching the bride eat her sample had prepared her taste buds for an almond cupcake.

"Have you met the doc?" Kerry asked.

Melody shrugged, grabbing a fork. "Maybe once. He seemed all right."

Kerry rolled her eyes. "Yeah, if you like your sweets with no sugar."

Leslie laughed at the analogy, licking cinnamon from her fingers as she ate her last bite of cookie. "It's not like you even know him, Kerry. Who are you to judge?"

"Well," Kerry said. "He's awful ... dull. And... I don't know.... There's just something else I don't like about him. Besides, I heard he didn't even do that well in medical school—that he barely passed. I've also heard that he was fired from his last position, and that's why he moved here. There's also a rumor that he is a shameless flirt and that his dismissal had something to do with that. The only reason he's here is because his father knew Dorinda's dad a long time ago. Sounds like he's more of a charity case than a doctor if you ask me."

"No one's asking, Kerry," Melody said, anxious to wrap up this conversation and get back to work on the cake. "Everything you've said is hearsay anyway. Dorinda is walking in a state of bliss, and apparently, she's in love with him, so I wouldn't worry too much. You're not the one marrying him."

"Yup," Kerry responded. "It's her mistake."

Melody retreated to the back as her assistants continued to banter about Dr. Werther. Still, Kerry's remark lingered in her mind. Between the maid of honor and the bridegroom, something just didn't seem right.

The whole affair had taken some of the joy out of creating the cake. After all, if the rumors were true and Robin was a womanizer and no good as a doctor, in the end, what difference would the appearance of the cake make? The thought so thoroughly disturbed Melody that she convinced herself it was best to put it completely out of her mind. With that, she returned to her work.

CHAPTER TWO

*M*elody rolled over, pounding the snooze button on her alarm clock with more force than necessary. She groaned, pulling her covers up closer around her chin. She'd been so absorbed with preparing for Dorinda's wedding while simultaneously keeping up with the demands of the bakery that sleep had been pushed aside. The effects of her busy schedule were definitely beginning to take a toll.

The wedding.

Suddenly, Melody's mind was fully awake though her body still protested at the thought of rising. She staggered to a sitting position, wiping sleep from her eyes, blinking owlishly as Smudge leaped up onto the bed, tongue out, tail wagging, and ready for a walk.

"You're far more ready for this day than I am," she muttered to her happy pup, rubbing her behind her ears. "This is it." There was no way she'd be able to go back to sleep now and enjoy it—too much to do. Besides, Smudge made it more than plain that she wasn't going to wait around any longer for her walk as she bounded off of the bed, racing to the front room and returning with her leash, tail wagging vigorously.

Once she was up, showered, and outside with Smudge, Melody began to feel better about the day. She and Smudge's walks down Main street provided her with the exercise she was unable to obtain otherwise due to her busy schedule, and on a day like this, she was more grateful for it than ever.

The pair walked at a brisk pace for nearly half an hour until Smudge finally slowed a little in order to drink water from a community dog bowl near one of the shops.

· · ·

Melody sat down on a nearby bench to rest. She took a deep breath, shutting her eyes both to soak in the sun above her and try to prepare her mind for the day ahead. However, her moment of tranquility was swiftly interrupted by an unfamiliar voice.

"Excuse me."

Melody opened her eyes to find a tall blonde man standing before her. At first glance, he reminded her a little of Fred from Scooby-Doo, a cartoon she'd loved as a kid. But this man appeared to possess none of Fred's charisma as his face remained decidedly serious as he spoke.

"Do you know where the Werther-Mitchum wedding is?" he asked.

"I certainly do," Melody said, rising. "In fact, I'll be headed there myself shortly. The ceremony will take place in the event hall at the end of the street. Just head north, and you'll run right into it. I don't believe I've met you before."

The man gave a nod, still not bothering to crack a smile. "Thank you for your help, much obliged."

Melody's brows rose in surprise when he turned on his heels and marched away, both ignoring her question and the laws of common courtesy.

"Nice to meet you, too," Melody murmured to herself. Smudge let out a restrained growl. "So, you had the same feeling about him as I did, huh, Smudge?"

Smudge agreed with a high-pitched bark just as Melody's cell rang. Alvin Henessy, the town sheriff, popped up on the caller ID. Though she was a bit hesitant to admit it, Melody had been growing steadily more attached to Alvin as of late and dared to hope that he still felt the same. She couldn't keep her heart from skipping a beat at the sight of his name, a phenomenon that was becoming quite common when it came to the sheriff. It was almost as if she was back in high school with a schoolgirl crush. The thought had her releasing a loud snort before she answered the call.

"Hey, Al," Melody greeted.

"Hi, Mel."

Melody could hear a smile in his voice, and it made her smile too.

"I called to remind you that I'm picking you up in two hours. Need help getting things loaded in your van for the wedding?"

"That would be greatly appreciated, thanks, Al."

"Great. I assume you're at home now doing all of your primping."

Melody laughed. "I'm afraid not. All of my attention is going to be on getting that cake and the rest of the food safely to the event hall. I couldn't care less what I look like." She paused only for a moment before she quickly added, "Don't worry, I won't look too shoddy."

"I wasn't worried," Alvin said.

"Okay, good. I wanted to make sure you knew you weren't going to end up with a hideous date."

Now it was the sheriff's turn to laugh. "You couldn't look hideous if you tried."

The comment created a brief moment of awkwardness, and Melody heard Alvin clear his throat on the other end. They were getting closer but weren't quite at the point where they could openly make such comments without at least slight embarrassment.

Thinking that the kind thing to do was to rescue him, Melody spoke first. "I appreciate your willingness to help with the food. I'll see you in two hours."

"See you."

"I guess it's time to really seize the day, isn't it?" Melody asked Smudge after hanging up with Alvin. She immediately dialed Kerry.

"Hey, Kerry. How goes it?"

"As well as can be expected on a day like this," Kerry answered, her voice flustered.

"Don't worry, I haven't deserted you. I'm just headed back from a walk with Smudge, and then I'll be over at the bakery."

"Get ready first if you'd like, we've got it under control for the moment."

"I did plan on getting ready first. I'll be over as soon as possible, though."

"We need you here, but don't rush so much that you neglect your looks."

Melody exhaled. "What's that supposed to mean?"

The stress left Kerry's voice for the moment, turning to teasing. "You know what I mean. Make sure you dress to impress. And I don't mean because of the wedding—I mean because of a certain sheriff we all know...."

Melody scolded Kerry for saying such things, but truth be told, she was feeling as giddy as a teenager already. Telling herself to focus and not let childish excitement get the best of her, she turned toward home, her mind tallying up last-minute tasks that needed attention.

Melody rushed to the mirror on the far end of her office when she heard the front doorbell of the bakery ring. She ran a hand over her hair and straightened out her emerald green chiffon. It was the first dress she'd bought herself in a long time, and she hoped it would be all right. She leaned in closer to make sure that the red lipstick she only bothered with on special occasions was just so and then made her way to the front, Smudge on her heels.

"Hi, Al," she greeted when she found him seated at a table in the front room. Melody hoped that her eyes didn't give away her feelings as she took in his appearance. She loved the way he looked in his sheriff uniform but thought he looked stunning in a dark blue collared shirt that brought out the color of his eyes.

"Hey, Mel. You look great!"

"Thank you." Melody turned away in the hope that he wouldn't notice the blush heating her cheeks. "Uh, the food and everything is back here."

She led the way to the kitchen, where Kerry had already arranged ice packs around all of the food.

"Hi there, you two," Kerry greeted, sending Melody a smile that was anything but subtle.

Melody wanted to smack her then and there for her lack of tact but instead focused on the task at hand. "Here it all is. Shall we get to it?"

"Let's do it," Alvin agreed, taking the box of sandwiches Kerry handed over.

Between the three of them, the van was loaded up in

no time. Kerry made a point of taking her own car, leaving Melody and Alvin with the van and some alone time.

Though Melody could have been annoyed with her friend's meddling, she had to admit she was excited to be one-on-one with Alvin before the craziness began.

The moment they arrived at the venue, it was all hands on deck as they plunged into the pre-wedding chaos.

Melody helped with the unloading before searching out Leslie, who had arrived first to guide the dining room setup.

"Hey, Les. How's everything?" Melody asked when she finally located her assistant.

Leslie looked up from the silverware she was busy laying out on one of the tables. Her face was flushed though she looked adorable, all dressed up for the wedding.

"It's going all right. This setup crew is pretty efficient, so that helps."

"Well, you know Doctor Mitchum," Melody said. "Nothing but the best will do for his daughter. She glanced around at the staff busily at work. "Where is the cake table?"

Leslie scanned the room. "I guess it still needs to be put out."

"Well, that cake can't just sit in the van," Melody pointed out. "I'll go see to it."

Kerry arrived just then, brow furrowed. "I can't find the special cake knife anywhere. Didn't you put them in the van, Leslie?"

"I've been here all morning!" Leslie retorted. "Are you really trying to pin something that fell under your responsibility for the day on me?"

"But I told you to put them in the van this morning when you were leaving!"

"Seriously, you two, not here," Melody interjected.

"It's not going to be fun making do with some

random knife from the kitchen," Kerry said. "Do you want your beautiful cake butchered?"

Melody waved her off. "Don't panic, I'll find it. And you two, if you could, please try to get along for once."

Kerry and Leslie nodded, reluctantly. Melody figured that had to be enough and turned away.

She made her rounds about the entire venue, ensuring that everything related to food was in order before asking about the cake setup. One of the staff-members quickly saw to it. Melody shook her head when she found the cake knife right in the front of the van, though Kerry had been too flustered to even notice.

"The knife has been found, and the table is ready for the cake," Melody told Kerry after finding her fussing over the drink table that would soon feature the bakery's homemade raspberry iced tea.

"Okay, good," Kerry said. "Are you going to head over to the church now?"

"Yeah, if you're sure everything is under control here.

It seems to be... I don't see why you can't come along now."

Kerry's eyes grew mischievous. "You and Sheriff Loverboy go ahead. Save two extra seats. Leslie and I will be over soon."

Melody tried to look stern but knew she failed miserably when Kerry only laughed.

Shaking her head, the baker made her way from the venue.

"Everything's under control?" Alvin asked as they turned toward the church, which was within walking distance.

"Seems to be," Melody said. "Now all we have to do is get through the wedding, reception and everything else. No sweat."

Alvin only laughed. "Yeah, no sweat."

CHAPTER THREE

The church was exquisitely decorated for the wedding. Classic love songs resonated in the crowded sanctuary, keeping everyone entertained while waiting for the ceremony to start.

Melody admired the flower arrangements, especially loving how well they matched her choice of floral design for the wedding cake. Guests mingled throughout the building, milling through the pews talking and finding seats. Melody didn't recognize any members of the wedding party. Perhaps they were all helping the bride and groom prepare. She glanced at her watch. It was already fifteen minutes after the wedding was scheduled to begin. She supposed it was normal for an event like this to be delayed a little....

"Where do you want to sit?" Alvin asked.

Melody glanced around, wanting to make sure she'd be able to exit the church before the throng when it came time to dash to the reception. "How about over there nearest the side exit. We'll still be able to see okay, right?"

Like a perfect gentleman, Alvin agreed to wherever she thought best and helped her save seats for Leslie and Kerry. Once seated, they waited for another ten minutes before Melody began to wonder if anything was wrong. The wedding was now a half-hour late, and there was no sign that it was about to begin.

"Something wrong?" Alvin asked.

"Just wondering why things haven't started yet....." She could tell that the attendees were becoming restless and questions that mirrored Melody's rippled throughout the room. It seemed to Melody that around now, the bridegroom should be present at the altar with his best man just waiting for the bride's arrival. Kerry's previous accusations against Robin on the day that Dorinda and Laurel visited the bakery popped uninvited into her head. Wasn't it usually the players who left their brides at the altar because when it came down to it, they couldn't make themselves commit?

Even as she told herself that she was surely jumping to conclusions, Melody turned to Alvin, already standing.

"Al, I think something's wrong. I'm going to go and find out what's happened."

"I'll go with you," Alvin said.

Melody nodded, gratefully. They moved swiftly out of the church and to the small bed and breakfast nearby that was reserved for the bride and groom along with their wedding parties.

"I didn't see a single member of the wedding party back there," Melody told Alvin as they walked. "I really hope nothing has happened and they are just running late....."

They crossed the street and entered the bed and breakfast where the wedding party stayed. The bridesmaids and groomsmen were all assembled in the lobby, waiting. An air of uneasiness permeated the room, causing Melody's stomach to drop as her suspicions were confirmed.

"What's happening?" Melody inquired of the room at large.

"No one knows," one of the bridesmaids answered, fiddling nervously with her bouquet.

"Robin has been missing for hours," a groomsman said.

All of a sudden, a piercing cry shot through the air, causing everyone in the room to freeze.

CHAPTER FOUR

*A*lvin shot into action, moving swiftly down the hallway toward the sound of the shout. At the doorway to Dorinda's room, he turned back, putting a hand out to stop Melody. "I'd better check on them first."

Melody wrung her hands impatiently in front of her as he slipped inside. Only a few moments passed before she disobeyed the sheriff's command and followed him.

The cries had grown substantially louder, and Melody's insides grew cold when she realized it was Dorinda who was now sobbing uncontrollably. However, what she noticed next was far worse... the groom!

Robin Werther lay in the center of the room..... dead. At least, it was safe to conclude that he was dead, considering the amount of blood that pooled around him and the fact that his skin was as white as snow.

"Dorinda, step away, please," Alvin ordered the trembling bride who sat crumpled next to her fiancé's corpse. With shaking hands and wobbling legs, she stood, stepping away. She almost dropped once more to the ground, but Melody reached her just in time.

"I'm so sorry, Dorinda," she said, only causing Dorinda to sob harder. She wrapped an arm around the distraught bride's shoulders and glanced around the room. "What on earth happened?"

"I did it."

Melody, Alvin, and Dorinda turned to the sound of Dr. Ambrose Mitchum's voice. A few moments of tense silence passed as the threesome stared wide-eyed at the bride's elderly father, all dressed in a pristine, white tuxedo. His face was pale as a ghost.

"No, Dad," Dorinda cried. "Don't say that."

Melody continued to hold Dorinda's shaking

shoulders, wracked afresh with sobs. The old doctor's eyes were rimmed with tears.

"I killed that man," he repeated. "I killed him because he didn't really love my daughter. The truth is, he was taking advantage of her. He was using her to build his career. I could not let anyone do that to my precious daughter! I should have stopped it before now, but I just couldn't."

"This is absurd," Melody muttered softly. "There's no way you could have...."

"You didn't do it, Dad!" Dorinda cried hysterically. Melody's heart broke for Dorinda and her father. She caught Alvin's gaze and easily confirmed that he too didn't know what to think of the situation.

Dorinda squirmed out of Melody's hold and went to his father. He caught hold of his daughter as she began to sob again.

"I'm sorry, Dorinda. I'm sorry!"

Melody watched the doctor closely, wondering at the fact that he was so quick to claim he'd just committed murder. Once again, something wasn't right.

"Dad, no. Please, you didn't do it. I know you didn't," Dorinda insisted.

"I have to bring you both to the station," Alvin said.

Dorinda and her father looked over at the sheriff with something akin to shock, as if they'd forgotten his presence completely. Dashing tears from her face with little regard for her carefully laid wedding makeup, Dorinda nodded. However, Dr. Mitchum wasn't quite so quick to agree.

"You don't have to bring my daughter. It's all my fault, Sheriff."

"Are you telling the truth, Doc?" Alvin asked. "Or are you protecting someone?"

"I'm not protecting anyone," Dr. Mitchum confirmed once more. "Just leave my daughter out of this, please."

"We can't accept your confession yet until we've investigated the situation further," Alvin explained, stepping aside, motioning for father and daughter to proceed with him from the room.

"I'm telling you, I'm the guilty one, and she has nothing to do with it!"

Alvin glanced over at Melody. When Dr. Mitchum embraced Dorinda once again, he crossed the room to speak with her. "I'm going to go and call the station. Will you stay here with them for a few more minutes?"

Melody nodded, mutely. Once Alvin had left the room, she angled away from the sight of the dead body, going over in her mind all that could have possibly happened. If Dr. Mitchum didn't commit the crime, then who did? And why was he so adamant that he was the guilty one? Poor Dorinda....

"More officers are on their way," Alvin said, snapping Melody out of her reverie. "I think now would be a good time for you to bow out."

Though she wanted to help, Melody obliged, readily.

This was too strange—it was best to let the law handle it from there. As she made her way down the hall, she tried to think up the best words to say to the bridal party, waiting to hear the news.

What a tragic way for a day that was supposed to be so joyous to start. Melody couldn't help going over, and over the misgivings she'd had during Dorinda's visit to the shop.... and Kerry's words about Robin...

even her color selection for the cake. Blue chrysanthemums had seemed far too innocent to her. What had she chosen instead? Red. Roses as red as blood on the hands of a murderer.

The bakery door felt as if it weighed 100 pounds as Melody pushed it open, stepping into the shop. The fact that the lights were on assured her Leslie and Kerry were already there.

"Hey," Melody greeted them as she entered the kitchen. Both Leslie and Kerry leaned against the counter, cups of tea in hand.

"Melody," Kerry immediately said, straightening. "Is it true? Is Dr. Werther really... dead?"

Leslie's eyes were as large as saucers behind her glasses as she waited for her boss to answer.

Melody exhaled, nodding. "Yeah."

Silence fell over the room.

"You want some tea?" Leslie finally offered.

"Sure." Melody joined Kerry by the counter.

"How was Dorinda?" Kerry asked.

Melody released a dry laugh. "How do you think?"

Kerry shook her head. "I just can't believe it. Are there any suspects yet?"

"Ambrose Mitchum claims he is responsible," she said.

Kerry's brow furrowed. "He just admitted straight out that he did it? But why?"

"It's a great question. Thanks, Leslie," Melody said, accepting the large mug of Constant Comment.

"What on earth did he say his reason was?" Leslie interjected.

Melody shook her head at the memory. "He said that Robin was only marrying Dorinda in order to further his career and that he couldn't let her go through with a marriage based on only that."

Kerry and Leslie exchanged a confused glance.

"I know, it's strange," Melody said, taking a cautious sip of her hot tea.

"Did you see his body?" Leslie asked, her voice hushed.

Melody nodded. "Al went to check on Dorinda when we heard loud cries from her room. There, we found the poor lifeless Robin at his bride's feet. He had what appeared to be a stab wound, but I didn't see a weapon around. Then, Ambrose came in and confessed to the murder."

"You were smart to take a police officer as your date, I guess," Kerry remarked though the morbid attempt at humor didn't elicit any response. "At least, there's no need to search for the murderer."

"There still might be. There's no proof yet that Ambrose is guilty."

"But, he confessed, didn't he?" Leslie said.

"That doesn't automatically mean he is. And I wouldn't be so quick to accept what the doctor is saying. Can either of you truly picture Ambrose killing anyone?"

Kerry and Leslie muttered that they couldn't, shaking their heads.

"There are lots of questions that need to be answered," Melody said.

"I, for one, am grateful that it is Al and his guys who have to do the questioning and not me," Leslie said, bringing her empty tea mug over to the sink.

"Can we head home now?" she asked. "I don't think I'd be able to work more today even if I tried."

Kerry and Melody agreed. "Kerry, I'll just close up shop and then give you a lift since you're on my way," Melody offered.

"Sure, thanks, Mel."

"See you all later," Leslie said, grabbing her keys from her pocket. "Try to get some rest."

"Yeah," Melody said, even as she determined that such a thing would be impossible. "You too."

CHAPTER FIVE

"*D*id you notice anything strange when you dropped off the cake?" Melody asked as she and Kerry got into the van.

Kerry shook her head. "The only thing I do remember is that none of the bridesmaids seemed excited when I saw them at the venue. They were all so quiet, like Laurel."

"So, it wasn't just Laurel?" Melody mused. "So odd."

They drove in silence for a few moments.

Melody looked out the window as they passed the church. The bridesmaids in their pink taffeta dresses were still outside the church, along with a few other guests. "I thought Al would have cleared everyone out by now."

"Hard to keep people from sticking around when something so drastic has just happened," Kerry remarked.

"Yeah...." Melody slowed the van down before pulling up to the curb and coming to a stop. "I think I'd like to have a word with one or two of them."

"Wait a minute, Mel," Kerry protested. "Didn't you just say that you're glad that it's the police who are investigating this and not you."

"No, it was Leslie who said that." Melody's seatbelt was already off, her hand on the door handle. "I, for one, want to know what happened, and this is the perfect opportunity."

Kerry looked concerned but eventually shrugged. "I'll wait for you here."

"Thanks, Kerry. This will be quick," she promised and got out of the car. She moved across the manicured grass, listening as the people around her offered their own unfounded speculations on Robin's untimely death. Melody offered solemn smiles to a few familiar faces, most of them customers from the bakery. After making her way through the onlookers, she made it to the bench where the bridesmaids were gathered.

"Excuse me?" she greeted.

All eyes turned to fix on Melody. She gave a small wave. "Hi, I'm Melody Marshall, the cake decorator."

Laurel nodded. "Hey, I remember you. Is there something you need?"

Melody paused, debating over the best way to glean information. The last thing she wanted was for the girls to think she was suspicious of them even though, at this stage, everyone was a suspect. "I just wanted to check on everyone. How are you all holding up?"

Laurel stepped forward as she took the liberty of speaking for the entire group before any of the other girls had a chance to speak up. "It's a little difficult to grieve for someone as vile as Robin Werther," she said.

Melody was taken aback by Laurel's fierce and

terribly blunt comment. "That's quite an accusation, Laurel. What makes you say that Robin was vile?"

Laurel sighed before speaking. "We all heard the rumors, Melody. I'm sure you did too."

Melody offered a slight nod.

"I know how Dorinda adored him, but I never liked the man. Especially after learning what he really wanted from Dorinda and how he behaved around women," Laurel explained.

A few of the bridesmaids murmured words of agreement.

Perhaps this was why Laurel had been so lackadaisical at the shop. If this is truly what Laurel believed of Robin, Melody could hardly blame her.

"Robin didn't deserve Dorinda. I will not shed any tears over his death. He has fooled many women, broken many hearts," Laurel said.

"Wow, that's really sad to hear," was all that Melody could say. "Is that how you all feel?" she added, remembering what Kerry said about the general lack of enthusiasm.

"We feel the same way Laurel does," one of them said. Everyone nodded in agrecment.

"He had a fling with one of my friends while he was engaged to Dorinda," another bridesmaid piped up. "The woman was so broken after I told her that he had a fiancé."

"I heard him bragging once to his friends about how lucky he was to catch an innocent fish like Dorinda. He said she would be the key to secure a position in the hospital," a fellow bridesmaid noted.

Melody would have thought nothing could shock her after what had already transpired, but she felt thoroughly overwhelmed by the bridesmaids' stories. If this was running in circles for a while, didn't anyone care for Dorinda? "If all of you felt this way, why didn't anyone think to warn Dorinda? Maybe this tragedy could have been avoided if someone had spoken up."

"Oh, most of us did, I assure you," Laurel said, "but Dorinda was too deaf to hear us. She was also too blind to see how Robin behaved with other women. She only wanted to see the best in him. I told her to leave the guy alone because it was plain to see that he was no good. But, instead of listening, she just kept on defending him. I don't know what kind of spell he cast on her. I guess that's why they say love is blind."

Everyone nodded in agreement, except for one petite brunette who kept her eyes on her lap as she fiddled with the wilting bouquet she still held in her hands. She looked even more heartbroken than the others and sat on the far end of the bench, separating herself from the other girls. The bridesmaids lapsed into their own conversation amongst themselves then, and Melody jumped at the opportunity to speak with the reticent brunette.

"Are you doing all right?" Melody asked. It seemed a bit redundant, but the girl had kept herself far from the conversation, so perhaps she hadn't felt included enough to offer any input.

The girl glanced up and nodded before looking back down at the bouquet.

"How do you know Dorinda?" Melody asked, sitting down next to the young woman.

"Dorinda's a friend of mine from back in our university days," she said. A sad smile came to her mouth. "We suffered through chemistry lab together."

"I see. What's your name?" Melody asked.

"Cathy Peck."

"It's nice to meet you, Cathy. I'm sorry about all of this. I'm sure Dorinda would be grateful to have you with her at a time like this. Perhaps you can see her once they're all finished at the police station."

Cathey nodded, looking close to tears. Her sorrow prompted Melody to ask if she was close to Robin.

Cathy tensed at the question. "Do I have to be close to Robin to feel this way? Doesn't he deserve someone to grieve for him? Is it also a crime to grieve for someone even though he was not that nice of a person?" Cathy asked.

Cathy's defensiveness was tangible.

"No. Of course, it's okay to grieve for someone. I'm sorry if it came out differently," Melody was quick to say. "It's natural to be sad when something so tragic has happened."

A moment of silence passed before Melody spoke again. "So, you only knew Robin through Dorinda?"

Cathy nodded. "Yeah, Dorinda talked about him all the time."

Melody hated to jump to conclusions, but she wondered if Cathy's genuine grief on Robin's behalf stemmed from some sort of deeper attachment that she wasn't prepared to disclose. Perhaps she had been one of his "women"?

"You really had no other... connection with him?" Melody ventured. The moment the words were out of her mouth, she wished she'd been able to figure out a more tactful way to phrase the question.

"What—what are you saying?" Cathy demanded, her proverbial bristles shooting back up again. "I hope you don't think that I... I mean, Robin and I...."

Melody waited on Cathy to find the right words, but the distraught bridesmaid only grew more flustered the more she tried. "I won't be accused of anything," she finally said, her voice taut.

Before Melody could contradict her statement, the

livid bridesmaid stalked toward the church without so much as a goodbye or a backward glance.

"Wow, okay," Melody said, feeling more suspicious than ever. She glanced at her watch, remembering Kerry before standing to bid the bridesmaids goodbye.

"Anything?" Kerry inquired as Melody resumed her place in the driver's seat.

"Did I find out who committed the murder? No. However, I did find out that almost everyone feels the exact way Laurel does about Robin."

"You mean that he was a no-good, manipulative womanizer?"

"Yeah, that." Melody threw the van into drive and steered away from the church. "Each bridesmaid had a story about why Robin was no good. Except for one...."

"Oh?"

"Her name is Cathy Peck. She seemed far more genuinely distraught. But if you ask me, she seems to be more upset about the loss of Robin than about what this whole ordeal has done to Dorinda...."

"Seriously?"

"She says that he deserves someone to grieve for him."

Kerry scowled. "No one has a heart big enough to feel sorry for that despicable character."

"Unless....." Melody ventured.

Kerry's eyes lit up with recognition. "Unless she had a deeper connection to him..... unless they were *involved*." She crossed her arms, her face contorted with thought. After a few moments, she shook her head, straightening up. "Okay, this is all very interesting, but I think you'd better leave things to the police from here on out. This is getting a little too weird, and I don't think you should be involved. None of us should."

Melody didn't promise Kerry anything. This was too weird..... and she wanted to get to the bottom of it as much as anyone.

CHAPTER SIX

*S*mudge was so excited to see Melody enter the house that she hopped around like a kangaroo as her owner set down her belongings. After the unimaginable stress of the day, Melody couldn't have been more grateful that she had such a happy little companion to come home to.

"Hey, buddy," she said, ignoring her fancy dress and getting right down onto her knees with the dog. "I'm sorry I was gone for so long. You wouldn't believe how this day turned out."

Smudge rolled onto her back, her mouth open, tongue hanging out of her mouth in a show of pure bliss as Melody rubbed her tummy.

Melody glanced down the hallway, but couldn't quite bring herself to turn in for the evening. "Tell you what," she told her dog as she stood to her feet and kicked off her fancy high heels. "We'll go for a walk. I think I need one as badly as you do."

It only took Melody a minute to change into yoga pants and hoodie. When she returned to the front of the house, Smudge was waiting at the door. She snatched up the leash, and the twosome were on their way.

Melody and Smudge walked their usual route. Melody was so lost in thoughts of the day that she didn't even notice Alvin's approach until Smudge released a few welcoming, high-pitched yaps in response to his nearness.

"Hi, Mel," Alvin greeted.

Melody released a breathless laugh. She couldn't tell if she was breathless because she hadn't realized Alvin was following them or simply because of his nearness in general. "Hey. Sorry, I must have been lost in thought."

Alvin shrugged. "Not surprised about that after

today. I was headed to your place to check in on you. How are you holding up?"

Melody stopped walking when she noticed that Alvin looked nearly as stressed as she felt. His earlier well-combed hair was a little rustled now, his eyes lined with worry. Still, Melody thought he was handsome, even in a casual outfit of jeans and a t-shirt. The attire suited his easy-going charm. However, the fact that he was worn out was unmistakable.

"It's been a long day," Melody remarked. Smudged jumped up and down at the sheriff's feet, eager for attention. They laughed, and Alvin leaned down to scratch behind Smudge's ears. "Let me take her for a while," he offered, taking the leash from Melody before they continued down the path.

"Are you getting closer to figuring out what really happened at the church?" Melody asked.

Alvin sighed, raking one large hand through his hair. "I don't think so, Mel. But, it's early yet so we'll keep trying. We'll need to test for fingerprints and uncover the murder weapon if the investigation is to go anywhere. I just hope that the murderer hasn't destroyed the evidence yet, whoever he may be."

"Or she," Melody added, wryly.

"Huh?"

Melody shook her head. "All I mean is that the murderer could be anyone at this point. There were so many people at the church and so many who didn't seem to like Robin Werther very much."

"You're right about that," Alvin agreed.

"So, what if the criminal did destroy the evidence?"

Alvin's mouth formed a distressed line. "It would be pretty difficult to pin down the murderer if that's the case, but not impossible. It would just take a little more work. With each day that passes, the chance of discovering the evidence lessens because the murderer has more time to cover his tracks. That's why my crew is going to be working non-stop on this case until justice has been served."

Melody watched Smudge prance contentedly in front of them, thinking. "What about Ambrose? Are you going to discount his claims simply because he admitted outright to the murder, which doesn't seem very... crook-like?"

"If Ambrose really did do it," Alvin explained, "he'd be able to produce the weapon he used. He hasn't done much in the way of hiding thus far, so it would be believable that he would still have the murder weapon in his possession. However, he hasn't come forward with it yet."

"But, should he decide to come forward with it, he would be convicted immediately?"

Alvin nodded. "If the weapon corresponded with the wound in Robin's chest and the rest of the evidence, yes."

Melody wondered if she should keep her interview with the bridesmaids a secret, fearing that Alvin might not approve of her meddling. Thinking, though, that perhaps the conversations she'd had were important, she decided against secrecy and took her chances.

"I talked with Dorinda's bridesmaids."

"About the murder?"

Melody nodded.

Alvin's expression was interested. "What did they say?"

Melody relayed the common distaste the girls held for Robin and also Cathy's peculiar reaction.

"Leslie and Kerry noticed early on that the girls didn't seem particularly thrilled about the wedding. They all seem to agree that he wasn't a great guy by any stretch and aren't exactly mourning his loss. Laurel, being Dorinda's closest friend, was the most vocal about her hatred for Robin."

"Who's Laurel?"

"Dorinda's maid of honor."

"Hmm. But Cathy seemed genuinely sad?"

"It seemed that way to me," Melody agreed. "She claims she had no direct connection to Robin, but grew very defensive when I pressed the point. I thought that maybe she'd once been an object of interest to Robin, but she wouldn't confirm anything."

Alvin's expression turned to one of amusement.

"What?" Melody demanded, stopping once again.

"I don't know why you're a pastry chef. I think you would do well as a detective," he joked.

Melody shook her head. "No, I just want to help."

Alvin chuckled. "Sure."

Melody shot him a look that was meant to silence him but only succeeded in making them both laugh. They continued on with their walk when Smudge started tugging impatiently on the leash.

"Just thinking out loud," Melody couldn't resist adding after only a few seconds. She saw Alvin attempting to hold his laughter out of the corner of her eye, but she foraged on.

"What if Dorinda was the murderer? I mean, Ambrose was so set on convincing everyone that he was the murderer, perhaps he was trying to protect his daughter. Perhaps Dorinda had begun to see Robin for the cad he was and decided to do him in before he could ruin her life."

"Anything is possible, Mel," Alvin agreed.

True though it might be, Melody desperately hoped that Dorinda wasn't the murderer. The situation was gruesome enough already, and she would hate to discover that sweet Dorinda had it in her heart to do something so terrible, no matter who the victim might be.

Melody was about to voice her concerns once more to Alvin when Smudge broke into a run, yanking Alvin behind him. Alvin and Melody laughed as they followed the dog right to the front of a local bar.

"She's on a mission," Alvin joked as they came to a stop. "Hey, what do you need from the bar, girl?"

Smudge led them in the direction of one of the outdoor tables where a man sat nursing a beer. It took Melody a while to realize that it was the mean version of Fred from earlier.

"Hey, Smudge, come over here," Alvin ordered. "We don't want to interrupt the man's—" he trailed off when Smudge released a low growl. Alvin looked to Melody in confusion.

"So smart," Melody murmured, amazed that Smudge recognized the surly stranger they'd met earlier.

"Who me?" Alvin asked.

Melody blushed, waving her hand at him. "No, not you, Smudge. I mean, you are smart, but...." It took her a moment to recover from the awkward direction the conversation had tumbled, but when she had regained her composure, she explained about her earlier encounter with the man. Before Alvin had a chance to stop her, Melody made a beeline for the man's table.

"Excuse me, sir?" she said.

The man looked up, his expression as far from welcoming as before.

"Hi, I believe we met earlier?"

No response.

It wasn't as if Melody was going to annoy the man any more than she was now, so she pressed her luck and continued. "Did you make it to the Mitchum-Werther wedding? I was there, but I don't remember seeing you."

"What are you talking about?" The man growled, his frown deepening.

"The wedding," Melody repeated. "You asked for directions to its location earlier today?"

"I don't know anything about that wedding," the man snapped, rudely, before taking a swig of his beer.

"But, you asked for directions...."

"I said I don't know anything about it!" he snapped again.

Apparently, he could get more annoyed, but Melody wasn't giving up. "So, you didn't make it?"

The man ignored her, taking another swig from his glass.

"Did you hear what happened? About the murder?"

Though the man was doing his best to ignore Melody's pestering, the blood in his face immediately drained at this question. His eyes widened at Melody's news.

Gotcha.

In the space of a heartbeat, the man leaped up from the table, obviously intent on abandoning Alvin and Melody as quickly as possible. His escape plan was thwarted when Smudge nipped at his ankles, causing him to trip. Alvin caught his arm, twisting it behind his back. The man grunted in a fury.

"Good job, Smudge!" Melody praised.

"What the heck do you think you're doing?" the man demanded.

"I'm sorry to disturb your afternoon like this, but the present circumstances demand that I question everyone connected to the disastrous wedding this morning. I'll need to take you in for questioning, and it would be a lot easier if you would cooperate. If not, I can always read you your rights and arrest you."

"I don't know anything about it! I didn't kill anyone!" he exclaimed.

Alvin held out his hand to help the man to get up. "I'm not saying you killed him. But I do need to take you in for questioning. If you'll just agree to work with me, you'll be on your way in no time. Do we have an understanding?"

The man stopped fighting back, though he scowled at the sheriff over his shoulder as he escorted him toward the road.

"Where do you want to take him?"

"If you don't mind, we'll head to the bakery since it's close."

Melody readily agreed.

Keeping a firm hold on the man, Alvin pulled out his radio. "I'm taking the liberty of questioning a man in the south end of town. It has to do with the murder case."

CHAPTER SEVEN

*M*elody unlocked the door of her shop, and Smudge bolted inside ahead of them. Alvin suggested they use her office, and she led the way.

"Sit down, mister," Alvin said in a commanding tone. The stranger sat down, but Alvin remained on his feet, ready to combat any escape attempt on the man's part. His strong arms were crossed in front of his chest, and he casually leaned against Melody's work desk.

"I'm not gonna say anything until I'm in the presence of my lawyer," the stranger said immediately.

Alvin sighed and looked at Melody. It certainly

wouldn't be easy to get information from the man. Melody tried to think of a way to bring his guard down. Perhaps if he thought an innocent woman was going to be put in jail.....

"Sir, if you can answer our questions, you could very well keep an innocent woman from going to jail," Melody said. She could feel Alvin's eyes drilling into her, demanding to know what on earth she was up to, but she kept her gaze from him and on the stranger only.

The stranger turned in Melody's direction. "Woman? What do you mean? Are you talking about Cathy? Has Cathy been accused?"

Melody met Alvin's eyes then, her brows rising in a silent "See?"

"If you are referring to Cathy Peck, one of Dorinda's bridesmaids, then yes."

The stranger was growing agitated now. "She isn't a suspect, is she?" he asked. Before Melody could ask the next question, Alvin did it for her.

"What is your name, sir?" Alvin asked.

"If I answer your question, will it keep Cathy safe?"

Alvin glanced over at Melody once again before nodding. "It will provide us with more information to find the person who is truly responsible for this crime and therefore remove suspicion from Miss Peck, yes."

"Okay, okay. I'll cooperate with you," he said.

"Let's start with your name," Alvin said.

"I'm Brad Mortimer."

"Mr. Mortimer, how are you related to Miss Peck?"

"Cathy—Cathy was my girlfriend," he said.

"*Was* your girlfriend," Alvin repeated. "You mean you are not together anymore?"

"Yeah." Brad averted his eyes. "We were together until that snake, Robin Werther, seduced her during his own engagement party."

Melody's eyes grew wide, but Alvin remained ever-calm.

"Go on," Alvin urged.

Brad exhaled before continuing. "My Cathy was fooled by Robin. She chose that slimy doctor over me even though she knew he would be getting married soon," Brad said with a tinge of pain in his voice.

A motive to kill? Melody certainly thought so.

"You asked me earlier where the wedding was, right?" Melody said. Though she'd been rather annoyed earlier at his curtness and lack of manners, she found it in her heart now to excuse his behavior. It couldn't be easy to lose his girl to a player like Robin.

"Yeah, I did," Brad acquiesced.

"If you hate Robin so much, why did you want to know where the wedding was? What were your intentions? If you are not with Cathy anymore, I assume you didn't have any business at the wedding ..." Melody reasoned. "Did Dorinda invite you? Are you part of the wedding party? Tell the truth, Brad."

Alvin motioned for Melody to back off. She crossed her arms, ignoring the sheriff, waiting for Brad to answer. Her interrogation technique was getting information out of the guy, so she figured if Alvin knew what was good for both of them and everyone involved in the case, he'd let her continue.

Brad thought for a full minute before responding. "I do admit that my initial goal was to confront Robin. I wanted to know why he just had to go after my girl when he was engaged to his own. I love Cathy more than anything, and he doesn't care one whit for her, but he stole her from me anyway just to show that he could."

It was obvious that Brad was fighting hard against his pent-up emotions, and another wave of sympathy toward him came over Melody.

"What time did you confront Robin Werther?" Alvin asked.

"I didn't." Brad's head drooped as he ran a hand restlessly through his hair. "I lost my nerve when I got to the church. I didn't even talk to him. But I did want to see Cathy. I hoped that maybe after Robin was married, she would change her mind and come back to me."

"So, she didn't change her mind?" Alvin inserted. "And you were angry about it and went to find Robin. What happened then?"

Brad rose from his seat. "I didn't kill Werther! I was angry with him, but I never thought of killing him!

Cathy hates violence, so even though that toad came between her and me, I would never stoop so low."

"Are you telling the truth?" Melody asked.

"Yes, I'm telling the truth! How many times do I have to repeat it?"

Melody looked over at Alvin, wondering what he thought of Brad's testimony. From his face, she couldn't tell whether or not he believed what the man said.

"Did you know that Robin Werther was murdered?" Melody asked.

Brad did not meet Melody's eyes. "I just heard."

"How did you hear about his death?" Alvin pressed on.

"From everyone. Everyone in Port Warren was talking about it. It would have been impossible not to hear the news. It was all over social media."

The tension in the room had continued to build and, at this stage, felt nearly suffocating. Alvin strode over to the mini-fridge in the corner of the office and pulled out three bottles of water. He motioned toward Brad. "Water?"

Brad hesitated for a moment before nodding.

Alvin clapped him on the shoulder after handing over the bottle. "I know this isn't easy, but you're doing well. I still do have a few more questions, but I want to thank you for your cooperation so far. Do you think you can hold out a little longer?"

Brad looked very much like he'd been put through the wringer, but he nodded.

Alvin handed Melody a bottle of water. She took it gratefully, just having realized how thirsty she'd become. Interrogation was certainly harder work than she'd imagined.

"Where were you an hour before the ceremony should have started?" Alvin went on.

Brad sighed. "I was outside the church. I wanted to approach Cathy, but she wasn't there. I just left and thought I'd try to find her after the wedding instead."

"Have you talked to her?" Melody asked.

"Yeah. After I heard what happened, I found her,

but she didn't want to talk. She was too upset about what had happened to that cheater."

Melody looked at Alvin, who seemed satisfied with Brad's answers.

"Mr. Mortimer, I want to thank you for your cooperation. You can go now, but that does not mean you are not one of the suspects, so the law does require that you remain in town. However, if you are not guilty, I assume that won't be an issue," Alvin said.

"Why am I still on the suspect list? I already told you I didn't do it."

"Everyone is a suspect. Please understand, Mr. Mortimer, you are in the same position now as everyone else who was anywhere near that wedding today. I ask that you simply bear with us while we work to get this all straightened out."

"I swear, I didn't do it. And I promise Cathy didn't do it either. I know her well, and I'm telling you she wasn't involved," Brad said.

Alvin nodded. "Okay, Mr. Mortimer, thank you. You're free to go."

Alvin escorted Brad out the door before returning inside to rejoin Melody.

"The list keeps getting longer," Melody said.

"That's how it happens sometimes," Alvin agreed, taking a drink from his water bottle. "It's especially difficult when any number of people could have had a good reason to kill the guy."

Melody nodded in agreement, and the room grew quiet as they were each lost in their own thoughts. A few moments passed before Melody looked up and found Alvin looking back at her. It wasn't until then that she realized what a terrible hostess she'd been. She had not offered him anything.

"My goodness, where are my manners? I have a kitchen full of goodies, and I haven't offered you anything after your long day. What can I get you, Al?" she asked.

"Oh, I'm fine, Melody," Alvin said.

Melody refused to take no for an answer. "Nonsense. What would you like? Tea? Coffee? And I have a variety of pastries, of course."

"I'll take whatever you have," Alvin said.

"Okay. I'll be back in a jiffy," Melody said, already making her way toward the kitchen.

Melody prepared some chamomile tea then brought out a slice of carrot cake from the fridge. She knew it was one of Alvin's favorites from her baking repertoire. She returned to her office and found Smudge in his lap. She smiled at the sight then handed him the slice of cake and mug of tea.

"You're going to sit down and dine with me, aren't you?" Alvin asked with mock formality. "After all, your day was as long as mine."

Melody smiled. "Yes, I believe I will." Somehow, in spite of the nightmare Dorinda's wedding day had turned out to be, she couldn't help feeling that this simple time spent sitting across from Alvin over carrot cake, and chamomile tea would make everything better.

CHAPTER EIGHT

*O*f course, life at Port Warren went on after Dorinda's tragic wedding day. Melody went right back to her usual routine in the bakery. Kerry and Leslie still constantly bickered amongst themselves over the simplest of things, and she was still called on to play referee.

Three days after the almost-wedding, Melody was elbow-deep in flour as she worked on the first of three items for Kerry's Aunt Rita. The old lady was fond of her baked goods and consistently featured them at the parties she hosted nearly every week. As usual, this week, Aunt Rita had ordered a pineapple upside-down cake, a hummingbird cake, and devil's food cake.

Melody was sifting the dry ingredients together when Kerry passed by.

"Hmm, that's Aunt Rita's order again, isn't it?" she remarked. "Why doesn't she ever order anything else?"

Melody waved her off. "Aunt Rita loves them, and it's her party. Besides, her friends on the charity board love these selections just as much as she does."

"Yeah," Kerry agreed, unenthusiastically. "Still, I think a little variety would do all of those old birds good."

Melody swatted at her assistant with a flour-coated hand. "Didn't anyone ever tell you not to speak about your elders that way?"

Kerry just rolled her eyes and moved on through the kitchen to the front room with her inventory list. After the craziness of the previous week, Melody had to admit that Kerry's incorrigible attitude was comfortingly familiar and therefore, quite welcome after all of the chaos, as was Aunt Rita's predictable order.

Just as she began dunking the thick pineapple slices

into simple syrup, the doorbell on the front door rang. As usual, Melody's heart skipped a beat when she recognized Alvin's voice as it mingled with Leslie's. She swiftly reached for a dishtowel, wiping furiously at her sticky fingers. She found it almost ridiculous that she wanted to smooth her hair and check her appearance in a mirror.

"Yoo-hoo, Melody!" Kerry called in a sing-song tone, popping her head around the corner. "You have a visitor."

"Ssshhhh, not so loud," Melody hissed.

Kerry only laughed. "He's a good guy, Mel, I don't know why you insist on being so secretive. It's not like the rest of us haven't noticed what's going on. The blind can see that you two are so into each other. So, just go on out now and greet your boyfriend."

"He's not my boyfriend," Melody retorted as she scrubbed her hands in the sink. Much as she wanted Kerry to think that Alvin's visit meant nothing to her, she couldn't help stopping to check her reflection in the mirror after removing her apron.

"You look good, Mel. You're always pretty, especially to Mr. Cop-man," Kerry said, her voice low.

Melody rolled her eyes at her friend, but couldn't quite keep the grin from her lips as she strode to the front of the bakery.

She greeted Alvin with a welcoming smile. "Al, so nice to see you this time of day. I didn't expect to see you until closing time." It was then that she noticed Alvin didn't appear completely at ease.

"Can we talk?" Alvin asked. His tone was far too business-like for this to be a social call.

"Of course. Why don't we go to my office?" Melody said.

Alvin nodded, following her down the hall. They sat next to each other on the long couch next to her work desk.

"What is this about, Al? You're making me nervous," Melody said. Alvin offered a small smile that made her feel slightly more at ease.

"Sorry, I guess I'm just focused."

If Melody hadn't felt so shy, she would have told

Alvin that she liked his focused face very much. Instead, she prompted him to continue.

"Ambrose and Dorinda Mitchum bailed out of jail this morning," he said.

This wasn't a huge surprise as the doctor had plenty of money at his disposal, making bail money a non-issue.

"They're out and about then," Melody said.

Alvin nodded. "The only condition is that they don't leave town, same as Mortimer."

Melody took this in, hoping Alvin couldn't tell that having suspects among them made her uneasy. "Any sign of the murder weapon?"

"Unfortunately, no. We double checked every corner of the bed and breakfast—all the rooms, the garbage, the kitchen... no sight of a weapon of any sort."

"I guess we'll just have to keep hoping that it's the next piece of evidence you find," Melody said, trying her best to be optimistic.

"I suppose so." Alvin stood then, glancing at his watch. "I can't stay, I just wanted to give you that update. Figured you deserve it after all of the help you gave me," he added with a smile.

Melody smiled. "It was nothing. Thanks for thinking of me, Al."

They walked out of the office, and Melody swung behind the counter to retrieve a box of cinnamon buns that she insisted he takes to headquarters.

"Thanks, Mel. I'll drop by again later if I get the chance," Alvin said.

"Don't worry about it. I know you're busy," Melody said. Smudge yelped in agreement, causing them both to laugh.

Alvin exited the shop then, and Melody returned to the kitchen, intent on finishing up Aunt Rita's order, but Kerry and Leslie had other ideas.

"So, what was that all about?" Kerry asked as she and her coworker strategically blocked their boss' way into the kitchen. "Did he ask you to marry him?"

Melody laughed as she ducked under her employee's arm, heading straight for the work table. She snatched up a piping bag and resumed her work, all the while, hoping that her cheeks didn't look as hot as they felt.

"What are you talking about? For goodness sake, we haven't even been..." What exactly had she and Alvin been doing? Certainly not officially dating — not yet anyway. "*Hanging out* that long. It was nothing like that. He dropped by to tell me that the Mitchums bailed themselves out of jail this morning."

"Oh." Kerry's hand flew to her tiny waist. "So, they can roam free in Port Warren? I don't like the thought of that."

"Me neither," Leslie agreed, squinting at Melody through her glasses. "What if one of them really is the murderer? What if the real criminal decides to stab everyone in town?"

Melody and Kerry shook their heads at the same time.

"They are not serial killers, Leslie," Kerry said.

"Quite right, Kerry," Melody agreed. "What happened to poor Robin was likely an act of passion. I doubt there will be any more gruesome stabbings."

"Well, I'm still worried." Leslie protested.

"I don't think the Mitchums are violent killers. They've always been nice people," Melody said.

"Except now one is a hardened criminal," Leslie pointed out.

"*Allegedly*," Melody interjected.

Leslie ignored Melody's comment and continued, "Trouble is, we don't know which one it is, so how are we supposed to know who to stay away from?"

Melody sighed with resignation. There was no point in saying another word on the Mitchums' possible innocence because clearly, everyone had decided one of them was guilty. The evidence against them was damning, though, and she had to admit that her employee had a point. If by chance, either Mitchum was guilty — *which* one was it?

Melody decided that she didn't want to encourage any more talk on the matter, so she let the subject drop and focused on the last touches on Aunt Rita's order. The angel food cake needed a little time to cool before delivery, which meant she had at least half an hour to kill.

"I think I'll stop by and see Dorinda before I make Aunt Rita's delivery," she announced to her friends as she removed her apron. "I'll be back in an hour or so."

The minute Smudge spotted Melody heading toward the door, she perked up. Figuring animals were always great comforters, she beckoned to the pup who was at her side in a moment, wagging her tail as Melody secured the leash to her collar. At the last minute, she grabbed a box of De Vine. It wouldn't hurt to arrive bearing every type of comfort possible.

As she walked, Melody tried to come up with what to say to Dorinda. It was difficult to know what to say to a woman whose world had just been smashed to smithereens. By the time she reached the Mitchum house, she still wasn't completely sure what the direction conversation should take. Figuring she'd mostly have to play it by ear, Melody reached up to ring the brass doorbell. Only a few moments passed before the door opened, revealing Dorinda on the other side.

"Oh, hi, Mel," she greeted with evidently forced enthusiasm.

Melody's heart went out to Dorinda as she observed the dark circles under her eyes and her pale face. Her hair was also unruly, a state in which Melody had never seen it. She was looking at a completely different Dorinda than the one who had been so bright-eyed and brimming with excitement just days before. Melody held out the box of De Vine. "I brought you a little something."

When Dorinda opened the lid, her eyes lit up in spite of her exhausted appearance.

"That's so thoughtful of you, Mel. Thank you," Dorinda said with sadness underlying her tone. "Come on inside."

Melody and Smudge followed Dorinda inside the house. It was Melody's first time inside the doctor's dwelling, and it certainly was exquisite. The walls were all white, and the expertly arranged furniture still smelled strongly of fine leather. Melody was invited to sit on the couch near the fireplace.

"How are you, Dorinda?" She inquired softly. Dorinda averted her gaze and Melody instinctively reached for her hand. "It's all right to be honest. I'm here to listen if you need to talk."

The kind words were apparently too much for Dorinda, and she immediately burst into tears. Melody squeezed Dorinda's hand as the other woman cried. "I should have listened to everyone! I'm so stubborn!" she sobbed around hiccups. "I shouldn't have accepted Robin into my life."

"You didn't know," Melody soothed.

Dorinda shook her head, vehemently. "But I did know. Just about everyone warned me, and I wouldn't listen. If I had listened, none of this would have happened." She covered her face with her hand, her shoulders shaking.

"It's not your fault, Dorinda. You did nothing wrong. You just trusted and loved someone. There's nothing wrong with that."

"But I was a fool! They were all telling me what a cad he was, and I still allowed myself to be beguiled by his sweet words."

Dorinda wiped tears from her cheeks with the back of her hand. Smudge jumped up onto the couch next to her, ready to offer comfort as well. Dorinda stroked Smudge's soft little head for a moment and even managed to smile down at the concerned pup.

"Mel? I don't know how to say this, but...."

"Go ahead," Melody encouraged.

Dorinda took a deep breath before continuing. "I hope you don't think I killed Robin. No matter what he did, I would never have the guts to kill anyone. Besides, I loved him. Even though he hurt me, I loved him."

"I believe in you, Dorinda," Melody comforted. "I saw the light he put in your eyes, and I would never question your grief when he died."

Dorinda started crying again as tears poured afresh from her dull, blue eyes. "I wish I could just forget all of it!"

"I know," Melody said. "How about your father? How is he?"

"I worry about him," Dorinda said, hiccupping. "He's old, you know. I'm afraid that this stressful ordeal isn't good for his health. I don't know what possessed him to take responsibility for the crime. My father couldn't bring himself to murder anyone any more than I could. he takes his oath as a doctor to do no harm very seriously, I assure you. He'd never hurt a soul."

"I know, I agree with you."

"My dad was as happy as I was the morning of the wedding," Dorinda went on. "He was excited about the wedding from the start. He thought the world of Robin and was eager to have another doctor joining the family. He would finally get someone he could play golf with and discuss boring medical stuff with."

Melody continued to listen as Dorinda's words tumbled forth in a rush.

"He was so excited yesterday. He even had his white tuxedo dry cleaned to make sure it would be perfect for my big day. He was so meticulous about the details of the wedding too. He wanted it to be such a success, Mel."

"I know, Dorinda," Melody said with a sigh. She reached over to grip the other woman's hand. "Don't worry. I talked to Al this morning, and he is working hard to get this whole mess straightened out. Now, I want you to just rest on that thought."

Dorinda offered a tearful nod as Melody stood.

"I need to make a delivery now. Smudge and I'll come to check in on you again, all right?"

Dorinda smiled as Smudge jumped off of the couch to follow her owner. She stood as well, pulling Melody in for a tight embrace. "Thank you for coming, Melody. You have no idea how much your visit means to me."

"I'm here to help. You'll let me know if there's anything I can do?"

Dorinda nodded, escorting her visitors to the door.

Though being able to comfort Dorinda should have made Melody happy, she instead found herself feeling even more uneasy about the murder than before. Dorinda was in such distress and would continue to be so as long as the investigation dragged on.

"Oh, Al," she murmured. "Please find that murder weapon soon. I don't know how much more waiting poor Dorinda can take."

CHAPTER NINE

The next day after another sleepless night spent contemplating the case of Robin Werther's murder, Melody heaved a sigh and dropped her head to her desk. She was going through photos, trying to build a portfolio of cake decorations for a birthday cake for one of her clients to choose from. She'd been at it for almost an hour, and the only thing she'd accomplished was to stare at one photo until the image started to blur.

Rubbing her eyes tiredly, Melody pushed her chair away from the desk and dragged her eyes from the computer screen to stretch her tense shoulder muscles. "I don't know why I'm so pressed about this case," she mumbled. "I'm not a detective, for goodness sake."

Smudge, sprawled in her usual corner, lifted one eyelid to cast her owner a curious glance before going right back to sleep. Melody snorted, a bit jealous of Smudge's relaxed attitude. How she wished she could be just as unruffled about the murder case. Especially as it really had nothing to do with her. It was just so difficult to let go of the recent tragedy because it was in *her* beloved little town and involved people she *knew*. People she considered friends.

Deciding that she would get absolutely no work done, Melody jumped up and marched through the door. The sound of paws scurrying behind her indicated that Smudge was now wide awake.

Rounding the corner into the kitchen, Melody found Kerry and Leslie huddled together. The women spoke in hushed tones, piquing Melody's curiosity. It wasn't often she found Kerry and Leslie doing anything other than bickering. The closer she got to the couple, she realized that Kerry was demonstrating how to make spun sugar while Leslie looked on raptly.

"Wow, this is a pleasant surprise," Melody mused. Two heads whipped around. "Seeing you two working together so peacefully is new."

Leslie's lips twisted wryly as she adjusted her glasses. "It sure is new. Kerry told me you taught her how to make spun sugar. I figured I'd ask her to show me rather than bother you. You seemed so focused on whatever you were doing when I peeked in your office."

"Don't get too excited, Melody," Kerry snickered. "I only agreed to teach Leslie so I can have it to rub in her face later."

"Could you be any more contemptible?" Leslie scoffed.

"No more than you," Kerry quipped with a wicked grin.

"Well, that didn't last long," Melody voiced before Leslie could respond and have world war three erupt in the kitchen.

Leslie grinned good-naturedly and turned to Melody. "So, boss, what were you so engrossed in earlier. You were staring at your computer with such intensity, I thought it would burst into flames."

Leaning against the counter, Melody huffed. "I was focused all right, so focused I didn't even see you. But, I wasn't concentrating on what I was supposed to be working on, gathering possible cake designs for Mrs. Charles to choose from for little Matty's birthday party. Instead, I was thinking about Dorinda's wedding that wasn't and her dead groom."

Kerry and Leslie exchanged knowing glances. "I told you she wouldn't give it up," Kerry muttered, tucking a lock of her stubborn hair behind her ear.

Melody directed pointed stares at her employees. She was annoyed that her inability to stay out of police matters had been discussed among them. "You're right, I can't give it up. On that note, I have a question."

"Shoot," Leslie said.

"Ambrose Mitchum was present when we delivered the cake, right?"

There was a long pause as both women

contemplated. Finally, Leslie nodded. "I got to the venue first, and he was indeed there."

"And he was present when we showed up later with the cake," Kerry confirmed.

Melody rubbed her chin thoughtfully. She'd thought she spotted Ambrose when she arrived with Kerry and Alvin as well but, she wanted to make sure. "He wasn't dressed for the wedding when we arrived, was he?"

Another moment of silence.

"No," Kerry and Leslie murmured in unison.

Melody nodded. "That's what I thought." Ambrose's tux hadn't a spot of blood on it, she remembered that much clearly. Perhaps it was possible that the good doctor had committed the crime before he changed. If that was the case, where were the clothes he had on before he changed into his tux?

"Ladies, I have to run out for a bit. Can I count on you two to hold things down here?"

"Of course," they chorused.

"Care to let us in on the epiphany you seem to have just had?" Kerry inquired, eyeing Melody with curiosity.

"Uh... no, not just yet." She didn't want to arouse further suspicion around Ambrose's name on the chance that the man really wasn't guilty. "Maybe later. There's something I have to check out first."

Melody hot-footed it back to her office to grab her phone and purse, eager to pay Ambrose a visit. She sent Alvin a text, letting him know her intention to question him. A response came in, but she didn't bother to check because she knew full well that Alvin wouldn't be in agreement with her confronting a suspect on her own. But, she just had to speak with Ambrose. The fire of curiosity had been lit inside of her, and the only way to put out the flames was with answers.

When Melody stepped into Ambrose's office, she was shocked to find the doctor in the process of packing. Glancing back into the lobby, it just registered that the room was empty. Not even the receptionist was present. Dr. Mitchum's office was in disarray with file cabinets flung open and files littering the massive oak desk in the center of the room and the floor. All of the drawers of the desk were wide open, and Ambrose was frantically scooping out its contents and dumping them into a briefcase.

The sinking feeling of Ambrose's possible guilt struck Melody. Swallowing, she stepped further into the office aware of Smudge standing quietly at her feet. The dog's eyes also followed the doctor's agitated movements with interest.

"Dr. Mitchum?" Melody called tentatively.

Realizing he had company for the first time, Ambrose started. "Melody, what... what are you doing here?" He peered over her shoulder, expecting to see the sheriff.

"I came to talk, but you seem to have... other plans," Melody answered. "Are you going somewhere?" Her eyes landed on his briefcase before flying back to him.

Ambrose pulled in a breath and immediately broke down. The older man's shoulders sagged, and he perched on the edge of his desk to massage the bridge of his nose. Despite his suspicious behavior, a wave of sympathy passed through Melody at the sight of his defeated posture.

"I'm leaving town, Melody."

"But, doing that will only make you look... guilty."

"I'm well aware," Ambrose shrugged. "But I might as well. No matter how this case turns out, my involvement guarantees that I'll no longer be accepted as the town's trusted physician. I'll no longer be accepted in this town period, and neither will my daughter."

Melody studied the man for a minute, wondering if he had intended to take Dorinda with him on the run. "That's not true, Dr. Mitchum. I'm sure once you're found innocent, things will go back to normal."

He shook his head slowly. "The suspicion alone has tainted my name for good, I'm afraid. Now, if you'll excuse me..." Ambrose rose to commence his packing.

Nibbling her lower lip, Melody thought long and hard about how to proceed. She couldn't allow a murder suspect to leave town. And, though the evidence against Ambrose was damning, deep down in her gut, she felt he was innocent. As if sensing her rising agitation, Smudge whined and rubbed against her leg. Melody reached down to rub the pup between the ears.

"Are you leaving town simply because you fear your name has been tainted, or are you feeling guilty about something, Dr. Mitchum?"

Silence.

Melody slowly lifted her gaze to Ambrose, all the while stroking Smudge's soft coat. The atmosphere crackled with rising tension as Ambrose stared at her with hard eyes that had suddenly gone cold. The warm, gentle man she knew seemed to have disappeared.

"You're so attentive to that dog of yours," he observed, taking Melody by surprise.

"Well..."

"One can say you love that bulldog as if she were your... baby."

Melody straightened, confused by the turn of conversation. She blinked and nodded. "Um... well, sure. I guess you could say that. What does that have to do with..."

Her eyes widened to saucers when Ambrose suddenly reached into the top drawer of his desk and held up no other than the missing cake knife.

CHAPTER TEN

aking an involuntary step back, Melody eyed the weapon in Ambrose's hand warily. It took her a moment to recover from her shock and regain her ability to form words.

"Dr. Mitchum, what are you doing with that?" There was something about his face that chilled her to the bone. "Don't do anything foolish," she warned. There was no telling what the man intended to do with that knife.

Ambrose stepped out from behind his desk, knife still in hand and wild eyes darting from the weapon to her. Melody took another step back and gulped. The situation she found herself in was not at all what she'd expected when she decided to pay Ambrose a visit. For a second, she regretted showing up at the man's office. Perhaps she should have brought Alvin along after all.

She sent Smudge a quick glance, noting that the dog stood at attention and bristled with menace. *Good.* It was a good thing her pup was always good at picking up on possible threats. The second she made a run for it, she knew Smudge would follow. And she was fully intending on skedaddling when Ambrose stopped his advance and heaved a sigh. Melody's heart rate slowed a bit at the sight of the doctor's less threatening stance.

"I met a man right before the wedding," he began.

Melody's ears perked up, much like Smudge's, and she raised her chin and nodded, willing him on. "Oh?" she managed. There she was in danger, and she just couldn't squash her curiosity. If she had a chance of uncovering what happened the day of Robin Werther's murder, she was sticking around.

Curiosity killed the cat, Melody, she reminded herself. Instead of doing the sane thing and getting herself out of her current situation, she heard herself say, "Go on."

"He told me his name is Brad Mortimer."

Instantly, recognition hit. *Mean Fred*. Although, after hearing Brad Mortimer's story, Melody had decided the poor man wasn't so mean after all. He was just... broken-hearted. "What does he have to do with anything?"

Ambrose's jaws clenched, and he stared at the floor for a while before getting back to his story. "There I was flitting about excitedly, trying to ensure that everything was perfect for my little girl's big day. I was so happy that she was happy and in love. I had already accepted Robin as family because he made my girl so happy. Plus, his father and I go way back." Ambrose laughed bitterly. "Then this Brad Mortimer tells me that Robin carried on with his girlfriend, one of Dorinda's bridesmaids. Apparently, the girl was Brad's girlfriend, and Robin swooped in and stole her away... while he was engaged to my little girl!

"He claimed the girl had fallen so badly for Robin, that she held on to the hope that they'd be together despite Robin's upcoming nuptial." Ambrose snorted and shook his head. "His fiancé's *bridesmaid*. Can you imagine the audacity of that... *scoundrel*? It wasn't hard to believe, considering the rumors that constantly swirled about Robin. I mean, I was fully aware of what people said, but I was reluctant to believe them. Reluctant to think of the pain it would bring Dorinda."

Ambrose stopped, and his eyes seemed to will her to understand. Melody nodded and smiled a little despite her fear.

"I've never been one to be too judgmental or accept rumors as facts without concrete proof," Ambrose continued. "I'd gotten to know the man, and he seemed like a good person, so I gave him the benefit of the doubt."

"That's understandable," Melody interjected with a small voice.

"Either I'm a fool, or Robin was an Oscar-worthy actor." He shrugged. "Perhaps both. Finding out about Robin's unfaithfulness to my daughter was devastating, and I knew it would kill Dorinda. She had stars in her eyes when she looked at that man."

Melody opened her mouth to offer her sympathies, but Ambrose continued.

"I wanted Robin to pay for manipulating me and making a fool out of my daughter. I hadn't planned to kill him, but when I saw him... I was just so angry..." His eyes met Melody's, and she couldn't look away. She had been held captivated by his story, and she hung on his every word, waiting for what he'd say next. "I stabbed Robin with this knife."

Melody was sure her jaw brushed the office's nice navy blue carpet. Perhaps her gut feeling of Ambrose's innocence was off. *Way* off. The man had just confessed to murder, and he held the alleged murder weapon in his hand.

Ambrose scrubbed his face tiredly. "After I killed Robin, I went in search of Dorinda. I had intended on grabbing her and leaving. We'd be far away before Robin's body was discovered. When I couldn't find her, I panicked and dressed for the wedding, hoping to divert suspicion. I continued searching for her after that, hoping to spare her the sight of Robin's bloody body... but I was too late."

Ambrose took yet another step toward Melody, the knife still in hand. This time Smudge released a growl and stepped forward. "What are you planning to do with that knife, Dr. Mitchum?" Melody asked, fully alert, and prepared to spring into action. Once again, her heart rate accelerated and adrenaline began to pour into her system. But once again, Ambrose did the unexpected.

He released a long breath and dropped his hand. "Relax, Melody, I have no intention of doing you any harm." He eyed Smudge, who was still bristling with menace and watching his every movement, with mild amusement. "I need to get a loyal and fierce companion like the one you have here," he muttered. "Well, I guess a furry companion is no longer an option since I'll likely be in prison for the remainder of my life."

Melody watched the man snatch a clear plastic bag from a box on the counter to drop the knife inside. He handed her the weapon. "Here, take it. I know you're close to the sheriff. Take it to him, tell him to check for fingerprints. If my confession wasn't enough, this should help to solve the case."

With shaky fingers, Melody took the bag from Ambrose. She inspected the weapon with disbelief and swallowed. "Dr. Mitchum, not that your confession isn't commendable. I mean, if you did indeed commit a crime, the right thing to do is to turn yourself in. But I have to ask. Why are you doing this?" It appeared he'd been ready to go on the run when she arrived. She wondered what had brought about the change of attitude.

Eyes brimming with remorse met hers. "This is all my fault. I brought that vile man into my daughter's life. If I hadn't accepted him and taken him into my practice, he likely wouldn't have gotten the opportunity to weasel his way into my daughter's heart. If I deserve punishment for anything, it's that."

"Now, Dr. Mitchum, you can't blame yourself for that. Dorinda is an adult. She chose who she fell in love with, not you."

He shook his head. "I asked you earlier if you love your bulldog there like a baby, and you said yes. I'm sure you'd take measures to protect your baby, Melody. That's what I'm doing, protecting my baby girl."

Melody stared at the doctor long and hard as confusion swirled in her mind. If he'd already taken measures to protect Dorinda, that is, by killing Robin, what else did he think he was doing to protect her?

"You know, I had fully intended on fleeing until you showed up, but I can't do it. I have to protect Dorinda. It's the least I can do for being a bad father."

Melody clutched the bagged weapon and chanced a step toward Ambrose. She was still confused but felt the need to comfort him. Patting his shoulder, she said, "You're nowhere close to being a bad father. And you're a good man, Ambrose. You're doing the right thing. Not many men would be brave enough to come forward like this."

She sighed and glanced down at the knife she held. "I suppose I should get this to the sheriff now."

CHAPTER ELEVEN

*M*elody felt like a child about to receive a lecture as Alvin simply stared at her with a mixture of outrage and disbelief. She shifted uncomfortably under his stare. When she could take his silence no more, she sighed. "Well, say something."

"I can't believe you confronted a possible murderer. *Alone.*"

Melody shrugged. "Smudge was with me."

On cue, Smudge lifted her head and barked.

With a shake of his head, Alvin gave both Melody and Smudge annoyed glances before inspecting the bagged weapon she'd handed him. "So, Mitchum claims this is the weapon he used, huh?"

Glad that Alvin had decided to forgo further reprimanding, she nodded. "He did."

"I'll get it checked out. We will get prints too, but as he passed it to you that is a foregone conclusion." Alvin glanced over his shoulder. "Don't go chasing any more suspected killers while I'm gone."

Melody's lips curled into a slow smile when she recognized the humor gleaming in his eyes. "I won't move a muscle," she swore.

Not much later, Alvin appeared. His unreadable expression left Melody a bit irritated. She was dying to know the results of the tests on the weapon. Did it confirm that Ambrose was the killer?

"Well?" Melody prompted. If she wasn't so anxious, she would have laughed when Smudge jumped up from her corner by the door at the sight of Alvin, as if she too couldn't wait to hear the results.

Alvin gestured for her to follow him outside as another person had walked into the precinct. "I'll walk you to your car."

Gathering her purse, Melody followed him outside. When she was sure they wouldn't be overheard by anyone, she pressed, "Don't keep me in suspense, Al."

Alvin stopped and turned to her, arms folded and wearing a stern expression. "You do know that I shouldn't be discussing this case with you, right?"

Melody's heart dropped. She hoped Alvin wouldn't get all tight-lipped on her now.

"But thanks to your sleuthing and your irresponsible action of putting yourself in danger, we've made a discovery."

Melody smiled sheepishly as heat filled her cheeks. "And out of appreciation, you're going to share what you've found with this helpful civilian?" She stared at him hopefully, eliciting a rumble of laughter. Melody blushed harder. She always did love the sound of Alvin's laugh.

"Of course, Ambrose Mitchum's prints were found all over the weapon."

She sighed. "Does that mean?"

"It means that we still haven't confirmed Ambrose's guilt."

"*What?*" Melody gaped at Alvin. A confession and fingerprints on a weapon and still nothing? "I don't understand."

Alvin let out a long breath. "Though Ambrose's prints were present on that knife, there was no blood on it, and based on the medical examiner's report, it wasn't the murder weapon."

For what felt like the hundredth time that day, Melody felt pure shock roll through her system. So much for solving the murder. "Well, that was... unexpected. So, what's next?"

"Next, I go back to the scene and search for that missing knife."

Melody's brows shot up. That sounded like searching for a needle in a haystack after so many days had passed, but she kept the negativity to herself. "Good luck. I'm sorry I didn't help much. I really thought I did."

"Of course, you did," Alvin quickly reassured. "I think we've taken another step forward, and we've most likely ruled Ambrose out as a suspect. Though, we have to wonder as to his motives for confessing."

"What!"

"I think the good doctor found the body, saw the cake knife on the stand, and took it in case his daughter became a suspect. He just presumed it was the murder weapon, it wasn't, that knife is still missing."

Unconvinced, Melody nodded, "If you say so. I'm going to get back to the shop. If I learn anything further, you'll be the first to know."

Alvin held her door open as she slid into her car. Smudge hopped into her lap to jump to the passenger's seat, and Alvin smiled. "Just promise you'll be careful, Mel. You too, Smudge."

The dog yelped in response, and Melody turned to Alvin with a grin. "Smudge said it, we'll be careful."

Melody strolled into her kitchen, where Kerry and Leslie were still hard at work. The women were so engrossed in their respective tasks, neither one of them heard her arrive. Leslie picked up a knife and expertly and playfully twirled it in her hand before sinking it into a freshly baked loaf of bread.

"Hey, guys."

Leslie jumped and twirled around. "Gosh, Melody, don't sneak up on us like that."

"Sorry, I thought you would have heard my car pull up."

"Sheesh, why so jumpy, Les?" Kerry asked, eyeing Leslie with raised brows.

"There is a knife-wielding murderer running around town. Pardon me for being a little spooked. You know, we really should start keeping that back door locked," she murmured absently before resuming her task.

"So, how did things go?" Kerry asked Melody.

"What things?"

Rolling her eyes, Kerry pushed her bowl of cake batter aside. "Oh, come on, Mel, don't play coy. Either you left to have an afternoon rendezvous with your boyfriend, or you were meddling in police business. So, how did it go?"

Hands on her hips, Melody tried her best to look stern. "First of all, Alvin is not my boyfriend." Not that she would mind if they did make things official. "Second, you know me well. I did, in fact, leave to meddle in police business."

"*And?* Has the murderer been discovered?" Kerry's eyes lit up at the prospect of juicy town gossip. "It was Dorinda, wasn't it? She probably caught Robin with another woman."

Melody held up a hand. "Slow down. No, the murderer wasn't caught, and all I can say is that the police thought they found the murder weapon, but it turned out that it wasn't. Now, the search is on for the real weapon. That's all I'm at liberty to say." If she mentioned anything about her encounter with Ambrose Mitchum, chances are the entire town would know about it before nightfall. Melody wouldn't do that to the Mitchums. She still thought they were good people.

Plus, her suspicion that Ambrose was innocent was back full force after discovering the weapon he'd claimed to have killed Robin with wasn't the murder weapon. Both she and Alvin knew he was covering for someone. Dorinda perhaps? The thought of the sweet, bubbly Dorinda being capable of murder was mind-blowing. Plus, Dorinda had sworn up and down that she didn't kill Robin. Was the woman that good of a liar?

Melody's thoughts were interrupted by Kerry. She held up a finger. "I think I know who killed Robin."

Both Melody's and Leslie's head snapped to her. "Who?" they chorused.

With a dramatic pause and a teasing smirk, Kerry announced, "I think it was... Leslie."

"Excuse me?" An outraged Leslie rounded on Kerry, knife still in hand.

"*Kerry*," Melody warned, "That's enough of your outlandish theories. This is no joking matter."

"Who says I'm joking? Think about it, Leslie was awfully irritated when she recounted how Robin had made a pass at her. Plus, she was the first to arrive at the venue for the wedding, she could have done it then. Let's not forget the case of our missing cake knife. There you have it, motive and means. So, Les, do you have a confession to make? Could you be the knife-wielding maniac?"

"Why, I'll show you knife-wielding maniac," Leslie fumed and stormed toward Kerry.

Melody stepped between them, sending Kerry a reprimanding scowl. "Leslie, calm down, I'm sure Kerry doesn't really think you committed murder."

"But think about it, Melody. Leslie could have stolen the knife and gotten her revenge on Robin, the rake."

"How could you even think me capable of such a thing?" There was a sliver of hurt hidden behind Leslie's anger and annoyance.

"Everyone's a suspect at this point," Kerry shrugged.

"That's right, so *you* could have killed Robin. You had an opportunity to steal the cake knife from the shop."

Melody groaned. "*Enough* you two. Bickering about every little thing like school children is bad enough, but I draw the line at throwing around murder accusations. Now is not the time to turn on each other. I'm sure neither of you had anything to do with Robin's murder.

There was a series of barks and huffs from Smudge as if she too was disappointed in Melody's employees. Just then, Melody's phone pinged, and she dug it out of her purse. She felt a rush of excitement when she saw Alvin's message. He was going to talk to Ambrose and wanted her to come along. The thought that she was spending way too much time investigating a murder instead of doing her actual job occurred to her, but she brushed it off.

She was enjoying her time out of the shop, and most of all, she liked seeing Alvin as much as possible. "Well, ladies, I have to run."

"*Again?*" came a chorus from Kerry and Leslie. Both women stared at her with amazement.

"Why did you even bother coming in today, Melody?" Kerry asked, shaking her head.

"Hey, I'm the boss," Melody asserted. "Besides, I'm so confident in the two of you that I feel comfortable leaving things up to you ladies." That comment awarded her two proud mega-watt smiles.

With a satisfied grin, Melody shuffled to the back door. "Smudge, you stay here and make sure those two plays nice."

Smudge whined her protest and watched with big sad eyes as Melody disappeared out the door.

CHAPTER TWELVE

*M*elody pulled into the parking lot of Ambrose's office, where Alvin was already waiting. She took a second to admire his tall, lean frame leaned against his sheriff's cruiser with his hands shoved into his pockets. Jumping out of her car, she strolled toward him with a smile.

"Al, I was surprised to get your text."

He shrugged. "Well, at the rate you're going, this is pretty much your case. I couldn't question a suspect without the lead detective."

Pursing her lips, Melody fought hard to hold back her giggle and failed. "Very funny. Are you sure you don't moonlight as a comedian?"

With a deep chuckle, Alvin pushed away from his pick-up. "In all seriousness, I thought I could get more out of Mitchum with you present. He did feel comfortable confessing everything to you *and* handing you the weapon he claimed to have used."

"Makes sense," she smiled.

As they walked to the office's entrance, Alvin said. "I hope I didn't take you away from anything important." He held the door open, and she stepped into the lobby.

"Not at all. I didn't get into any work when I got back to the shop. I just chatted with the girls."

"I see you left your trusty companion. Where's Smudge?"

"At the shop, babysitting Kerry and Leslie."

That got another hearty laugh from Alvin, and she grinned broadly. Their amusement faded, however, as they neared Ambrose's office door. "I saw his vehicle still in the lot, I hope he's still here."

"I think he took leaving town off of his mind when I last saw him. I think he's still holed up in there."

Melody was right. Ambrose's office door swung open when Alvin twisted the knob, and there was Ambrose sitting calmly behind his desk.

"What took you so long, Sheriff?" Ambrose asked nonchalantly. "Good to see you again, Melody."

Melody and Alvin exchanged glances. "Dr. Mitchum... you're still here. How are you doing?" Melody inquired.

"As good as I can be considering the circumstances. So, Sheriff, I assume you're here to arrest me." Ambrose rose and offered his wrists. "I'm ready when you are."

Alvin's brows rose. "The thing is, Ambrose, I have no grounds to arrest you."

"Wha-*what?*" Ambrose's shocked gaze swung to Melody. "I thought you gave him the knife!"

"I did, but it wasn't the murder weapon," she confirmed softly.

A series of emotions flickered across Ambrose's face, confusion, disbelief, relief, and then disappointment. With a groan he sank into his wingback chair. "How is that possible?" he whispered more to himself than his guests.

Alvin stepped forward, his tone gentle. "Ambrose, I think it's time you tell the truth. Are you covering for someone? Your daughter, perhaps?"

All color seeped from the older man's face, and Melody feared he'd pass out. His eyes swung from Alvin to Melody and back again. Finally, fearful eyes landed on Melody. "You know my Dorinda, Melody. She's a good girl."

Melody glanced at Alvin, who nodded his encouragement. He'd been right to take her along. Apparently, Ambrose found it easier to talk to her. She took a seat in front of the desk, her expression sympathetic and her eyes filled with compassion.

"I do, Dr. Mitchum. I've gotten to know Dorinda over the course of planning her wedding. She *is* a sweet woman. That's why you need to tell the truth so we can help her. Keeping secrets and trying to cover things up will only make the situation worse in the long run, especially for her."

The doctor's eyes gleamed with unshed tears. "The

truth is... I think Dorinda is responsible for Robin's death."

"So you're *not* sure?" Alvin drew closer and perched on the edge of the desk.

"Go on, Dr. Mitchum tell us what happened," Melody encouraged.

Ambrose scrubbed a hand over his face. "I found Dorinda over Robin's body and fearing that she killed him, I went in search of the weapon, hoping to get rid of it before the police arrived. I mean, she appeared grief-stricken but the thought that she had killed him and was experiencing remorse crossed my mind. My first instinct was to protect my daughter. I found the cake knife. There was no blood on it, but I thought she could have wiped it clean. So, I took it and wiped it down. I ensured that only my prints were on that knife."

Alvin and Melody gawked at Ambrose. Alvin sighed and began to rub his temple. "And the plot thickens," he muttered. "Ambrose, did your daughter kill Robin or not?"

"I don't know." Ambrose threw his hands up. "I honestly don't know, but when I walked in on her kneeling over his body that was my first fear." Hope flickered in the man's eyes. "But now that there's no murder weapon, there's nothing linking my daughter to the crime except suspicion. She's free."

"If Dorinda is guilty, evidence could turn up," Melody voiced.

"Well, prosecute *me*! I confessed. Leave Dorinda out of this."

Alvin stifled a groan. "I'm afraid that isn't how the justice system works, Ambrose. "All right, I'll have to take you in. Let's go," he sighed.

Melody could hear Alvin's reluctance. She watched, feeling horrible as the doctor was marched out of the office and placed in the back of the police cruiser. Fortunately, there was no one around to see the doctor in such a compromising and undignified spot. Although, it wouldn't be long before word spread like wildfire when someone spotted him at the station.

"Oh, Alvin, what a mess," Melody sighed. "Thanks for not cuffing him. He really is a good man."

"I know. Ambrose is harmless. Unfortunately, I have

to do my job and charge him with obstruction of justice."

Melody nodded her understanding. "What now?"

"Now, you go home and get some rest. *Detective,*" Alvin teased. "You've been working this case more than my officers.

Melody stood by her car and watched Alvin drive off. For a while, she just stood there, going over everything she knew about the case in her mind. It was even harder to picture Dorinda as a killer than it was to picture her father as one. Something was definitely amiss, and she intended on finding out what.

Resolute that she would stay on the case regardless of it not being her job, she got into her car and headed back to the shop.

CHAPTER THIRTEEN

The next day, as soon as she got the chance, Melody went to the police station. Of course, it was almost dusk because she'd had to make a few deliveries for scheduled events, and then she decided to walk to the station so both she and Smudge could get a good workout.

The instant she walked through the door, she was greeted by a few officers.

"Hey, Melody, you sure have become a frequent visitor at this place," Rick Myers said. "Not that I'm complaining. You're easy on the eyes," he added with a wink.

"Watch it, Myers, That's the sheriff's woman," Jane, the secretary, declared.

Melody felt heat creep up her neck and spread to her face. She was sure she resembled a fire engine by the time the teasing was over.

"Hi, Melody, how's it going?" That was Abe Sinclair, a burly, sweet-natured man. "Why don't I see a box in your hand? Each time you visit, you should bring treats. I thought we'd established that." He smiled to let her know he was only teasing, but hopeful.

"You're the last person who should be demanding *treats*, Abe," Jane said, eyeing the man's round, protruding belly.

Melody smothered her laughter. "I'm here to see Alvin. Is he in?"

"He sure is. Go on around back," Jane permitted.

Melody found Alvin leaned over his desk, pouring over documents. "Knock knock."

He swung around and realizing who it was smiled. "Hi."

"Hi, Al."

Smudge sprang toward Alvin, tongue lolling as she was treated with a nice rub between the ears. "Hey there, Smudge. Good to see you too."

Melody watched man and dog interact with satisfaction. She loved that Smudge adored the man she hoped to get more involved with.

Alvin straightened. "I knew you wouldn't stay away for long. Come for an update on the case, detective?"

"Maybe I just came to see you," Melody challenged.

"Uh-huh."

Alvin laughed when she huffed and admitted, "All right, I was curious about the Mitchums' fate, and I *did* want to see you as well." She'd spent another sleepless night thinking about Dorinda and Ambrose.

"Well, the good doctor is still in custody... but we've got nothing on the daughter yet." Alvin shrugged. "I wish I had more than that to tell you. I'd really love to solve this case."

Leaning against the door, Melody harrumphed. "You know what I've been thinking?"

Giving her his full attention, Alvin perched on his desk and folded his arms. "That we should have dinner soon?"

Taken aback but pleasantly surprised, Melody flushed. "Sounds to me like you're asking me out."

"I am. Unfortunately, I'm bogged down with a murder case. I just thought I'd put it out there for you to consider."

Melody tucked a lock of hair behind her ear and smiled timidly. "I'll most certainly consider it." She didn't bother verbalizing that there was nothing to consider. She'd like nothing more than to have an official first date, since their original first date, the wedding, had ended with a murder.

Alvin's lips kicked up into a small smile. "So, what were you really thinking?"

"Well, I was thinking about Dorinda and how happy she was before her wedding. I honestly don't think she's guilty, Al. I think everyone was right, Dorinda was completely blinded by love, and whenever she talked about Robin, she made him sound like her white knight in shining armor, for goodness sake. And I was thinking about the knife that disappeared from my shop. I've had so many people come in, it's impossible to pinpoint…"

She paused when two big hands came down on each of her shoulders.

"Mel, I think you're way too stressed over this entire thing. Let *me* worry about it."

She sighed. "It's just that…"

"You care about the parties involved, and you're the sweetest woman I've ever met." Alvin finished with a smile.

Melody smiled back and staring up at him, she said, "Thank you for understanding and thanks for the compliment."

"We'll get to the bottom of this, Melody. I promise."

"All right. I should get going. Smudge and I walked here to get some exercise. I want to get home before it gets too late."

"I can give you a lift."

"No, I'd hate to take you away from work. You were obviously in the middle of something when I arrived." She nodded to the files spread across his desk. "Besides, Smudge and I didn't burn nearly enough calories. The walk back will do us good. Come on, girl, we're heading home."

Peeking out from the spot she'd found under Alvin's desk, Smudge stretched and sauntered to her owner.

"See you two later," Alvin said.

Melody enjoyed the cool night breeze as she and her dog slowly made their way home. It was one of those nights when the temperature was just right, and the streets were quiet. They only passed a few other pedestrians who offered quick greetings and smiles.

The only sounds were the soft whisper of the wind and the jiggling of the tiny bell around smudge's collar. "It's a lovely night for a walk, isn't it, girl?"

Smudge woofed and continued her trotting ahead of Melody.

When they neared the site that Dorinda's wedding was supposed to take place, a wave of sadness rolled through Melody. She stopped to stare at the building, lamenting on how what was supposed to be a joyful day ended in tragedy. If Dorinda and Robin had made it down the aisle, they'd be on their honeymoon now.

Melody's frown deepened as she contemplated what Dorinda's life would have been like being married to Robin. If he was capable of sleeping with her friend while they were engaged, Dorinda would have been in for a world of heartache. Still, as callous and unfaithful as Robin was, the man didn't deserve to die... and certainly not so horribly.

Just as she was about to continue walking, the sound of a bottle shattering on the pavement echoed. Melody's heart leaped as she surveyed her surroundings. Other than the gruesome stabbing that occurred days before, the town was fairly safe. Peering into several dark alleys was daunting, however.

Smudge's low growl was even more cause for alarm. Melody followed the dog's gaze as she continued to growl. A figure, shrouded in darkness emerged from around a corner, and Melody's breath hitched in her throat. The figure advanced toward the streetlight until Melody could make out who it was.

She let out a breath, relieved that she wasn't about to get mugged. It was Laurel Bauer, the woman who had acted as Dorinda's *unenthusiasti*c maid of honor.

"Laurel?"

The woman glanced up and squinted. "Yeah. Who's there?" She swayed, causing Melody to approach her.

"It's Melody Marshall. I made the cake for Dorinda's wedding."

"Oh, right. You're that nice baker lady. How's it going?" Laurel's words were slurred, and the closer Melody got, the stronger the scent of alcohol became. Clearly, Laurel was wasted.

"Are you all right, Laurel? What are you doing out here alone?"

"Just out for a walk like you and your four-legged friend there."

Smudge sat on her haunches, her eyes trained on Laurel, following her every move. It wasn't the fact that Laurel was heavily intoxicated that interested Melody. It was the fact that the woman's eyes kept darting to the street gutter parallel to where they stood.

When Melody stepped around the woman to see what she kept looking at, Laurel hurriedly blocked her path, raising further suspicion. Melody couldn't imagine what was so interesting about a gutter. She moved again, trying to get around Laurel, but she got the same reaction.

Laurel giggled nervously. "So, uh, Melody, what's been going on? I haven't seen you since the wedding... that didn't happen," she added with a snicker.

Melody's brows elevated. Laurel spoke as if they'd been well acquainted before she stepped into her bakery. She'd never met the woman before Dorinda introduced them, and she wanted to know what she'd been up to? With a lift of one shoulder, she replied, "I've been... baking."

For some reason, Laurel found that hilarious. The woman cackled. "Of course, because that's what you do. You bake beautiful cakes, by the way."

"Thanks," Melody said dryly. She was about to try again to maneuver around Laurel to see what she was hiding when Smudge began to bark excitedly. Only then did Melody realize that her dog had dashed behind Laurel and was peering into the gutter.

"What is it, girl?" Melody managed to get around Laurel because, in her drunken state, she staggered when she tried to stop Melody.

"No, wait!" Laurel protested.

Melody was already inspecting whatever caught Smudge's interest. The street light gave her a glimpse of something shiny resting in the gutter. Whipping out her phone for added light, Melody was shocked to see what Laurel had so desperately wanted to hide. It was a knife! One eerily similar to the one that had gone missing from her shop! There it was laid in the gutter. The blade was stained with blood. Melody's stomach lurched as she slowly turned around.

"Laurel, is that..."

Melody only realized that Laurel had pushed her when she hit the ground hard. In her inebriated state, Laurel moved with surprising speed to grab the knife from the gutter while Smudge's barks pierced the night as she circled her owner with concern.

Melody's eyes widened, and her dread mounted when Laurel pointed the knife at her. "Why couldn't you just mind your own business?"

CHAPTER FOURTEEN

Swallowing hard and annoyed that she found herself staring down a knife yet again, Melody slowly lifted herself from the ground. She held both palms out. "You don't want to do anything crazy, now do you, Laurel?"

Smudge snarled, keeping herself between the two women.

"Tell that dog to shut up," Laurel hissed. She glanced around to see if anyone was watching. "All of that barking will draw attention."

Good, Melody thought. She could use a rescue right now. But, since Laurel's agitation increased and she held the knife higher, Melody reluctantly tried to calm Smudge down. "It's all right, girl. It's all right. Easy."

Smudge's barks gradually decreased to low menacing growls.

"You take it easy as well, Laurel. There's no need to point that knife at me."

To Melody's surprise, Laurel's shoulders began to tremble, and she dropped her hand with a loud sob. "Oh, please. I don't want to hurt you. As if I'd want to add to my body count," she wailed.

A chill ran down Melody's spine.

Add to?

"What are you implying, Laurel?" Though the woman no longer pointed the knife threateningly at her, Melody still kept her distance.

Laurel sobbed harder, her shoulders drooping. Dashing away a tear, she said, "I thought getting revenge would make me feel better."

"I don't know what you mean," Melony said, but she was beginning to have an idea.

"Oh, what the hell, I might as well come clean.

Robin was *mine*."

Melody's jaw slackened. Robin was with Laurel too? The man just kept getting more despicable in her eyes.

"He wasn't seeing Dorinda long before I met him. I knew it was low to pursue my friend's boyfriend, but he seduced me. I was sure he was serious about me because we clicked, you know? I made him happier than Dorinda ever could. I know I did. He told me he loved me, and he promised that once he secured his spot at Dr, Mitchum's practice, he'd dump Dorinda and marry me. The things he said and did were so romantic... I was head over heels in love with Robin. He was so charming and handsome. I fell hard and fast."

"But didn't you feel sorry for your friend?"

"It was hard seeing him with Dorinda."

Melody nodded. The woman had at least felt some guilt.

Laurel shrugged. "I took comfort in the fact that he loved *me*. He was just using her, and when he got what he wanted, he'd get rid of her, and we'd start our life together." Laurel's expression darkened, and she all but snarled. "Then, I found out that he had proposed to Dorinda."

Or perhaps not, Melody felt her skin prickle at such selfish words

"I wanted to rip that ring from her bony finger when she showed up at my place so excited. Taunting me, she was! She kept waving it in my face. I nearly gagged when she demanded I be her maid of honor."

Melody threw her arms up. "Well, why didn't you say something then?"

The woman let out another sob. "I thought Robin was still stringing her along. I never thought he'd actually go through with the wedding. I figured he went that far to get in good with Ambrose Mitchum, and I didn't want to ruin his plans, so I played along. I mean, he kept coming to see me after he proposed to Dorinda, and he constantly told me I was the one he loved. I'm such a fool."

Melody swallowed. "So you...killed him?"

"Yes." The word was spoken so softly, Melody nearly missed it, but there it was — a confession from

Robin's killer. "I stole that knife from your shop the day Dorinda dragged me along to see her precious dream wedding cake. I got so angry, I grabbed the knife and hid it in my handbag, intent on stabbing *her* with it when we got back to her car."

Melody gasped, and Laurel shrugged. "You have no idea how difficult it was to help Dorinda plan her wedding with *my* man. It made me physically ill sometimes."

"What happened on the day of the wedding?" Melody asked.

"Well, I kept that knife I stole, obviously. It just so happened that it ended up in Robin's chest instead of Dorinda's. I confronted the scoundrel in his dressing room. When I asked him if he was really going to marry Dorinda, he said he was. *She's rich and well connected,* he'd said. And he had to honor his promise to Dorinda's father to make his daughter happy. I asked him about honoring his promise to me, and he laughed in my face. I was so angry... I guess I just lost it."

Laurel seemed far away, lost in thought. "Next thing I knew, Robin was on the floor in a pool of blood.

Realizing he was dead, I felt this sick sliver of satisfaction. he broke my heart, so I broke his — literally."

Oh my God.

Melody couldn't believe what she was hearing. Well, she could, but it was so surreal, like something out of a movie. "There wasn't a trace of blood on your dress," Melody mused aloud.

"I wasn't wearing my dress when I offed Robin. In a panic, I stashed the knife in my bag along with my bloody clothes. My clothes are still in my bag," Laurel laughed. "All of the evidence kept right there in my apartment under my bed. Foolish, right?"

Melody just continued to gawk at the woman. It wasn't often that she was struck speechless, but she had no idea how to respond to Laurel.

"It wasn't my intention to cause suspicion on Dorinda, but when it happened — when everyone started speculating that she did it — I was happy. She'd pay for stealing Robin from me by rotting in jail. I thought I'd be happy. I'd got my revenge." Laurel shrugged. "But I feel worse every day. I especially felt bad when poor Dr. Mitchum confessed. I had nothing against him," Laurel explained. "He's a nice man. God, that Dorinda just gets the easy way out every time, doesn't she?"

Melody glanced at Smudge, taking comfort in her companion's proximity. "If you go to the police and confess, maybe they'll be lenient. I can go with you, maybe..."

Hysterical laughter filled the air. Laurel cackled and lifted the knife to stare at it. "You're kidding, right? I stabbed a man in cold blood and almost sent two innocent people to prison. I've had the police on a wild goose chase for days. I'm thinking they're going to be mighty peeved and throw the book at me." She shook her head as she stared at the knife that she still clutched tightly. "There's only one way out of this for me, Melody."

Melody felt an ice-cold fear slide down her spine, and all she could do was stare. What would happen to Smudge? What about the bakery, would it survive? She would never find out if Alvin was the wonderful man she imagined!

Still deep in thought and loss, she stared wide-eyed as Laurel lifted the knife... to her own throat.

CHAPTER FIFTEEN

*M*elody felt an instant rush of adrenaline when she saw Laurel lift the blade to press it against her own throat.

"There's only one way out," she repeated.

"Laurel, no!" Melody bolted forward, not sure how she garnered such momentum so quickly. Miraculously, she reached Laurel before she could sink the blade into her skin and tackled her to the ground.

Melody tried to wrestle the knife from Laurel's grasp, but the woman's grip on the weapon was impossibly tight. They rolled around on the pavement in a tangle of limbs. "Let go and leave me alone," Laurel hissed. "I'm not going to prison. I can't."

"I refuse to let you kill yourself," Melody spit out as they wrangled on the ground.

Laurel managed to push Melody off of her. "What do you care?" She lifted the knife to her throat again, but Melody dove on top of her, and they proceeded to tussle. All the while, Smudge circled the women, jumping and barking. When Laurel got the upper hand and pinned Melody to the ground, the pup sprang into action, thinking that Melody was the one Laurel intended to hurt with the knife.

Smudge caught Laurel's wrist between her teeth and applied pressure until the blade fell from her hand. Laurel let out a howl of pain and grabbed her wrist, giving Melody the chance to knock her to the ground.

"Stupid dog!" Laurel spat, still clutching her wrist.

Rolling to a sitting position, Melody kicked the knife out of Laurel's reach, at the same time, trying to catch her breath. "That dog just saved your life. You would have killed yourself."

"It isn't like I have anything to live for at this point."

With an irritated huff, Melody patted Smudge's head. "Good job, girl. I'll give you all the butter cookies your little heart desires when we get home."

Smudge licked Melody's hand in response and kept watch as her owner crawled to Laurel. The woman slowly sat up, her lower lip quivering. She looked so forlorn and lost that Melody felt sympathy flood her. Sure, the woman just confessed to murder, but Melody couldn't help feeling sorry for her. After everything she went through with Robin and then the guilt she lived with after killing him, it had to be overwhelming.

"Don't talk like that, Laurel. I'm pretty sure death is never better." She took the woman's wrist to inspect it, but there was no real sign of damage. The gentle gesture sent Laurel into another episode of uncontrollable sobbing.

"Why are you being so kind to me after what I did?"

Taking her into her arms, Melody cooed, "There, there now. You made a horrible mistake. We all make mistakes."

"I'm sorry if I hurt you," Laurel sniffed.

"You didn't. I'm fine."

"I'm sorry for everything," Laurel wailed. "For being a horrible friend to Dorinda, for killing Robin. "I don't know how my life came to this. I deserve to die for everything I've done."

Smoothing Laurel's hair, Melody tightened her arms around the woman's shoulder. "No one deserves that, Laurel," she said softly. Following her owner's lead, Smudge padded forward to nuzzle Laurel's side in a show of comfort.

Melody didn't know how long they all sat on the sidewalk, but she gave Laurel time to get herself together. The woman sobbed until the only sounds coming from her were hiccups and occasional sniffs.

"Laurel?"

"I'll go," she blurted. "I'll go to the police station and confess... if you'll go with me."

Relief flooded Melody. She didn't think she had the strength to force Laurel to go to the authorities. "Of course, I'll go with you."

"I'm just so tired," Laurel added. "I'm ready for the nightmare to end. I'll do the time. I deserve to."

Giving her one more comforting squeeze, Melody helped Laurel to her feet. She then retrieved her phone, which had scattered out of her hand when she'd been pushed. Then, she picked up the knife. "Let's go, Laurel."

The journey to the police station was made in silence. The entire time, Melody wondered what was going through Laurel's mind. She never asked, fearing just one word would send the emotionally fragile woman into another spiral.

When they walked through the door of the police station. They were greeted with shocked stares. Melody could only imagine the picture they made. Laurel's eyes were puffy and red-rimmed, both of their clothes were disheveled, much of Laurel's short bob had escaped its ponytail. Melody was sure her mane looked like a bird's nest, and both women sported smears of dirt from rolling around on the ground. And there was the fact that Melody held a blood-stained knife in her hand. That got her a few horrified glances.

It was Alvin who rounded the counter and broke the stunned silence. "Melody? He performed a slow sweep of both women and then glanced at the dog who stood beside them. "What in the world happened?"

Smudge released a long whine and flopped down to cover her eyes with a paw. It would have normally incited laughter if Melody wasn't so utterly tired and a tad traumatized. "Do you think we can take this to your office?" she asked.

Alvin's mouth opened and closed several times before he gestured to them to follow him. Melody plopped on a chair and listened as Laurel recounted every detail of how she'd killed Robin and why.

In the end, Melody held up the blade. "This is the murder weapon, which my prints are now all over because I had to wrestle it out of Laurel's hand."

"*Wrestle?* Please explain," Alvin begged, staring at the knife.

"I tried to use it to kill myself," Laurel replied, lowly.

Alvin shoved a hand through his hair and gave Melody a reprimanding look for putting herself in danger. *Again.* She shrugged, and he grabbed a plastic bag from his desk. Melody dropped the weapon into the bag glad to finally get it out of her hand. The thought of holding on to a knife with a dead man's blood was becoming increasingly uncomfortable.

As Alvin led Laurel out of his office to be booked, Melody rested a hand on her arm. "You did the right thing turning yourself in, Laurel. I'm proud of you."

Laurel forced out a wobbly smile and nodded.

A while later, Alvin returned to his office to find Melody seated, her head resting against the wall, and her eyes closed. Smudge was at her feet, asleep, apparently as exhausted by the night's activities as her owner.

"Mel."

Her eyes open and she rubbed her face and sat up. "Hey, is..."

"Yes, Ms. Bauer is now behind bars, and Dr. Mitchum has been cleared to go home."

With a long sigh, Melody stood up. "Well, the case has been solved, Sheriff. Well done."

Alvin stared at her with a mixture of censure and adoration. "I don't know whether to lecture you or kiss you," he blurted.

Mouth hanging open, Melody gave a slow, owlish blink. Alvin had never been so forward with her before, and she didn't hate it. Surprising herself, she said, "I'd... I'd prefer the kiss."

And that was precisely what she got.

Alvin released her and chuckled. "I'm taking you home this time. Knowing you, you'll run into another murderer wanting to confess."

A slow smile lit up Melody's face. "Oh, don't be so dramatic."

Alvin chuckled as they exited his office with Smudge close on their heels. "You certainly do make my life more interesting, Melody. I suppose we can finally have that dinner date."

"I suppose we can," she affirmed. She smiled up at him. "If things stay quiet in town for a while, that is."

"I'll keep my fingers crossed.

CHAPTER SIXTEEN

ne week later, Melody was back to baking and finding the perfect cake decorations to fit each client's event.

"I'm thinking a full, extravagant bouquet made with buttercream on a white backdrop for Mrs. Crosse's birthday cake. The woman is obsessed with all thing's flowers. What do you think, Smudge?"

Smudge barely lifted her head and one eyelid in response.

"I get it loud and clear, girl. You don't care." Melody laughed as she made a note of the idea for Mrs. Crosse. "I'll see how she likes that idea later."

Next, she wheeled her chair around to study her calendar, which was filled with colorful sticky notes of the various upcoming events she'd be catering for. "Goodness, we've got a busy month ahead. Business is looking up." Jumping up, she stretched and strolled to the kitchen to check on Kerry and Leslie's progress.

They had dozens of macaroons, strudels, and eclairs to make by that evening for Mr. Mayfair's retirement party. Mr. Mayfair said he wanted enough pastries to give him diabetes by the end of his party because he was determined to leave his boring desk job with a bang. The memory of the man's direct orders made Melody chuckle.

"I think that's a great idea," Kerry gushed as Melody entered the kitchen.

"Isn't it, though?" Leslie clapped. "I'm so excited. You'll have to help me with the decorations. You're great at that sort of thing. You've got a real eye for color schemes."

"Thanks," Kerry smiled.

"What are you two planning?"

Both women turned. "Hey, boss," Leslie greeted. "We're planning my sister's going away party. She got her dream job in New York."

"Isn't that exciting?" Kerry squealed. "I've always wanted to go to New York. When Leslie's sister is settled at her new place, we're both going to visit. And the party we're planning to send her off with is going to be epic."

Melody watched, amazed as the two high-fived across the counter. "Okay, what have you done to the real Kerry and Leslie?"

Leslie stared at Melody innocently behind her glasses. "Whatever do you mean?"

"I haven't heard any bickering from you two in days, and now you're planning a party together. Not only that, you're planning a trip to New York. *Together*. I'm happy you two seem to have grown up but *what* happened?"

The girls exchanged long looks, and Kerry shrugged. "Well, after what happened with Robin Werther... then with Laurel snapping and turning into a crazy killer... we've decided that bad blood between people leads to *deadly* consequences. Pun intended."

"Laurel wasn't crazy," Melody defended.

"Exactly," Leslie pointed out. "But she did something crazy because of all that pent up hate. It was either Kerry and I got along, or we'd end up killing each other. We chose to get along."

Amused, Melody nodded. "Well, I'm glad that something good came out of the tragedy. How are you guys doing with Mr. Mayfair's order?"

"We're making good time," Leslie said.

"Yeah, now that we spend less time arguing, we move a lot faster," Kerry chimed in.

"Awesome," Melody murmured.

The sight of the sheriff's cruiser pulling up in front of the shop put a broad smile on Melody's face. "Ladies, carry on. I'm stepping outside for a bit." Both Kerry and Leslie gave her knowing smiles.

"Sure," they sang in unison.

"Smudge, come here, girl. Al is here."

Seconds later, Smudge skidded around the corner, tongue hanging out and tail wagging excitedly. Her leash, still attached to her collar, dragged behind her.

The dog was out the door ahead of Melody and racing toward Alvin. When Smudge saw Alvin or even heard his name, Melody was sure it meant playtime to the pup. Shaking her head as she approached, she watched Smudge roll over, and Alvin automatically stooped to scratch her tummy.

"Hey, girl," he laughed. "It's always nice to see you too." Alvin glanced up to see Melody approaching and stood up. "Good morning."

"Good morning, Al. What a pleasant surprise. What brings you by?"

"I stopped by to tell you what an amazing time I had at dinner the other night," he drawled.

As was typical, heat flooded her face. "I did too. And you stopped just to tell me that?"

"Sure, and to ask you if we could do it again soon somewhere more intimate like your place or mine."

Melody's heart skipped a beat. Yes, that meant they were officially a couple. "Sure," she breathed. She couldn't remember the last time she'd had someone at her place for *anything*.

"Great." Alvin rocked back on his heels. "I've got some time to burn right now. Were you busy?"

"Not at all."

"What do you say we take Smudge for a walk around the block?"

She nodded eagerly. "Sounds good."

Alvin picked up Smudge's leash, and she skipped ahead. Boldly, Melody laced her fingers with Alvin's. He grinned in response, and they began their stroll.

"So," Alvin began. "I bet you've been dying to know how things turned out for everyone in the Robin Werther case."

Shaking her head, Melody feigned nonchalance. "I haven't dwelled on the matter much. However, if you wish to share a few details, I won't mind."

Alvin gazed down at her with a smirk. "In other words, you've been dying to know."

She let out a huff. "All right, you got me. *Yes.* Tell me everything."

Alvin threw his head back and roared with laughter,

making Melody smile. She reveled in the deep sound resonating through her.

"Well, surprise, surprise, Dorinda has decided to speak on Laurel's behalf at her trial."

Melody gasped. "Really? My, that's incredible of her. After everything, Dorinda still has the heart to forgive her friend. I just knew she was a good woman."

"Indeed," Alvin agreed. "She's a better person than most. You'll be happy to know that Ambrose Mitchum is back at his practice. After his innocence was declared, the town decided to overlook the entire debacle."

"As they should. Dr. Mitchum is an incredible physician. I'm so happy everything worked out for him."

"Me too," Alvin said. "Would you believe that Cathy Peck and Brad Mortimer have made amends?"

Melody glance up. "You don't say? How do you know?"

"Cathy stopped by the station to see Laurel and Brad

was with her. As soon as they were both free to leave town, they did just that."

"Look at that, a happy ending for at least one couple."

"Just one?" Alvin grinned, gazing down at their connected hands.

Melody let out a girly giggle. "Okay, more than a few people got a happy ending." She sighed. "It's still so tragic that what was supposed to be a happy affair ended in bloodshed."

"I certainly hope the next wedding that comes to Port Warren is a more joyful affair."

Melody glanced up and found Alvin gazing down at her with an unreadable expression. She stopped, and so did he. "Another wedding in Port Warren," she mused. "Yes, I'm sure that one will be a much happier affair." Seeing the intent in his eyes as he stared at her mouth, she reached up to give him a quick kiss.

Looking around, Melody realized that they stood across from the park. "So much for a stroll around the block." She hadn't taken notice of the distance they'd walked because she'd been so caught up in Alvin and their conversation.

He smiled and pulled a tennis ball from his pocket. "I couldn't go back to work without a quick game of fetch with one of my favorite girls. Isn't that right, Smudge?"

Smudge practically did backflips at the sight of the tiny green ball. Melody watched man and dog play with a feeling of contentment and the biggest smile.

STRAWBERRIES AND SWEET LIES
PREVIEW

If you missed the first book in this amazing cozy series, read on for a preview...

Ding. Melody stretched the dough a little further; holding her breath as she expertly pulled it just enough to ensure a perfectly thin, translucent layer. The bell pinged again, and Melody glanced around for Kerry.

"Hey, Ker—where are you?" she called, failing to detect her assistant's presence. Melody shook her head, wiped her hands on her apron, exited the kitchen and hurried into the shop. There stood her best customer, Alvin Hennessy, the small town's local sheriff, his kind brown eyes lighting up as

Melody came into his view. He hastily removed his hat, cleared his throat and smiled sheepishly down at her.

"Oh, hey there, Mel. Sorry to stop in again today, but I forgot I needed a cake for Ma's hen party tonight." Alvin shuffled his feet shyly, his cheeks reddening.

Melody sighed. She was grateful for his business, but suspected he purposely cut his order in two so he had an excuse to drop by twice today. She would have preferred efficiency, but good manners and a genuine fondness for the sheriff prevented her from showing any exasperation. She should be flattered by his attention—she knew, but she really wasn't interested in a romantic relationship at this point in her life. Not that he wasn't handsome, in his own way, but he was just not her type, she supposed, even if she *were* in the market for a romantic relationship. She took a quick moment to evaluate his appearance. He possessed the long, lean lines of a thoroughbred, but somehow wasn't able to project his inherent attractiveness, even in uniform. Perhaps it was his somewhat elongated face, but no, that wasn't really it; it was more his inability to realize his own appeal, a slight insecurity, an awkwardness. She mentally shook herself and focused on the business at hand.

"Not a problem, Al. Always good to see you!" she said, forcing a genuine smile.

She felt a pang of guilt at her fib, but knew she probably made his day with her comment. In spite of her uncanny ability to notice and discern the overt as well as hidden attributes of others, Melody possessed a baffling blindness to her own qualities. She could have easily graced the pages of any girlie magazine, even in jeans and her trademark logoed tee. An Irish beauty, Melody was blessed with more than her fair share of pluses: glossy auburn, shoulder-length tresses (albeit piled on her head and anchored with a hairnet), an angelic face, and statuesque curves to rival any pin-up girl. She had many secret (and not so secret) male admirers in town, but even though she was consistently friendly and courteous, she possessed an intimidating blend of self-assurance, the formerly discussed unawareness of her beauty, and a steadfast personal rule against flirting.

"What kind of cake did you have in mind? We have a cream cheese-filled red velvet and an orange-hickory nut on hand. Kerry made them yesterday, and they're still fresh."

As if summoned by her name, Kerry rushed in, flinging out hyper apologies as she whipped on an apron over her uniform of sparkly blue jeans and the shop's logo-emblazoned t-shirt.

"Where were you?" Melody asked.

"I forgot my phone in my car and wanted to make sure Aunt Rita didn't call with her family reunion order. I told her to call the shop rather than my cell, but she never remembers the number and can't be bothered to look it up. Good thing I checked; as she did leave me a voicemail with what she wants, and she's hoping to get everything tomorrow afternoon, even though the reunion doesn't start until Friday evening!" Kerry's words tumbled over each other as her hands gestured wildly. Melody wondered how Kerry was able to breathe while talking at such a rate.

"I see you've gone over your quota of caffeine today," Melody teased, noting Kerry's messy blond bun slipping out of the hair net stretched crookedly over her head and the slight sheen of sweat on her brow.

Kerry, plump and pretty, was engaged to Port

Warren High's beloved football coach, George Stanley, who adored her. In Kerry's mind, this gave her free reign to play matchmaker with all her unfortunately single friends and acquaintances, especially her beautiful boss.

"Yeah, might have overdone the go-juice just a tad." Kerry chuckled, tucking her stray blond strands back into the net. Kerry then turned her attention to their visitor. "Hey, Al, you forget something? Weren't you in earlier?"

Alvin blushed and nodded, looking down at his shoes and rubbing his close-cropped brown hair.

Kerry smiled wickedly at his obvious discomfiture. "I'm beginning to think this is your new office!"

Melody gave her a quick, pursed-lip glare, knowing it would only encourage her would-be marriage broker to continue to tease poor Alvin.

"Yep, completely forgot about Ma's card deal tonight; she wanted me to pick up a cake; whatcha got in stock?" Alvin asked trying to recover himself.

As the sheriff switched his embarrassed attention to

his torturer, Melody took the opportunity to slip quietly back into the kitchen to finish the croissants, leaving Kerry to fill Alvin's order. She concentrated, cutting and folding thin strips into perfect crescents.

"That guy's got it bad!" Kerry announced as she sailed into the kitchen, automatically beelining it for the coffee machine.

"No! You're cut off!" Melody was quick to see her assistant's intention and she grabbed Kerry's sleeve with a floury hand, "No more coffee for you!"

Kerry sheepishly set the pot back down and crossed her arms. She eyed the tray of bakery rejects that failed Melody's perfectionistic eye, sighed, and helped herself to a broken cookie. Nibbling, she glared at Melody.

"You've got it bad," Melody insisted. "You're torturing that poor man, and you know it! What did he end up buying?"

"Don't try and change the subject! That dog is one whipped puppy. If he really forgot that cake this morning, I'm a one-eyed frog. His mom has bridge every Wednesday night, tonight is no exception!"

Kerry exclaimed while munching through a second cookie reject.

Melody shrugged, not wanting to encourage that line of thinking. She'd known for a while that Alvin had a thing for her. She tried her best to ignore it and avoid him as much as possible. With her busy schedule, she just wasn't ready for anything serious, even if it was with someone like Alvin. Or was it really about her schedule? Whatever, she was just not into a relationship at the moment. She had to admit, he was a good guy. And he would probably treat her right if she ever gave him a chance. But it was just too soon.

"He's either going to have to man up and ask you out or go broke buying donuts and cakes! For a lawman, he ain't very brave!" Kerry added.

Melody let her rattle on, hoping Kerry would run out of words on the subject, though that seemed unlikely.

Kerry propped her chin on her left palm looking all dreamy. "I think he's cute, though, don't you? A little on the puppy dog side, but still pretty manly when he's not tripping over his tongue when you're around."

Melody sighed, rolled her eyes, and kept silent. It was her weapon of choice and it worked well with Kerry, whose main hobby was verbalizing, combined with taking off on frequent, caffeine-infused rabbit trails. So, Kerry prattled on while Mel took a moment to mull over the situation.

In truth, she almost wished she reciprocated Alvin's apparent feelings. She dreaded the day she would really have to reject such a nice guy. She blew out a breath of frustration, hoping against hope that he would never find the courage to approach her romantically because in that way she could avoid the whole ordeal. If he did ever find the courage to ask her out, she would just have to find a nice way to turn him down. Maybe she should start thinking about how she could get out of it without hurting his feelings.

Her thoughts, generally practical, quickly switched over to Aunt Rita's reunion and she broke into Kerry's monologue.

"Which cake did the sheriff end up buying? And what does Aunt Rita need by Friday?" Melody asked and Kerry cooperated with the subject change, her talking talent showcased by her ability to jump off and on any topic train.

"He decided on the red velvet. Auntie said she needs three cakes: one devil's food, one pineapple upside down, and one hummingbird. I think I should call her and steer her away from the hummingbird, as it's too similar to the pineapple upside-down—don't you think? Maybe a pecan Texas sheet instead? Add a little variety? Also, she wants two-dozen each of chocolate chip, shortbread and peanut butter cookies, an apple strudel and six dozen dinner rolls. I think I better tell her to freeze everything when she gets it tomorrow since she's not serving most of it until Saturday and Sunday, and I wouldn't think she'd like them anything but fresh. Really, she should get everything from us Friday afternoon; we could have it done by two, don't you think? Maybe I should call her? Maybe not, as she never changes her mind once she makes a plan; maybe you should call her? She'd probably listen to you better than me. But maybe freezing them would be good enough and then we wouldn't be as stressed on Saturday, as we have that wedding cake to deliver and set up, and Jeannette isn't somebody we want to disappoint with shoddy work..." Kerry continued to ponder the quandary of her aunt's order while she bustled about wiping counters, putting away clean tools from the dish drainer, and checking—and double-checking—the stores of supplies.

Just then the bell dinged, heralding another customer, and Kerry whisked out of the kitchen.

Melody opened the oven and placed the croissant trays inside, setting the timer as she finished. She could hear Kerry's voice, presumably talking to a customer, and while tempted to start on tomorrow's orders, she knew she should make an appearance in the shop as some of her customers took it very personally when she was too busy to greet them.

Kerry's Aunt Rita stood at the counter, her lips pursed as she listened to her niece's flood of advice. Rita held up her hand, finally getting Kerry to slow her word flow. Aunt Rita had a closet full of old-fashioned, 50's style dresses that belted at the waist, everything from floral, to stripes and plaids, to plain. She only ever wore dark brown, laced up walking shoes, white gloves, and netted hats whenever she ventured outside her house. Inside, she wore button-up housedresses, ones she deemed suitable for the constant cleaning she inflicted on her house. Dust was terrified to land anywhere in her vicinity.

"I need everything by tomorrow afternoon, Kerry Ann, is that going to be a problem?" Just as Kerry opened her mouth to answer, Rita caught sight of Melody.

"Thank God you're here! My niece seems to think I don't know my own mind, and I need her to understand that I need everything tomorrow afternoon. I will be extremely busy with other reunion tasks... of course, I have to do everything myself, the rest of the family cannot be trusted... so I need the desserts squared away tomorrow. Is that too difficult?" Rita glared at Melody belligerently.

"Oh no, Rita, tomorrow afternoon is perfect! We don't have another big order besides yours due until Friday afternoon, so it will work out just fine, and your choices show nice forethought and variety," Melody assured her.

"Hmph. Kerry Ann here seems to think I don't have enough variety in the cake department. I keep trying to explain that Cousin Harold loves the pineapple upside down and my sister must have hummingbird.

There is no room for substitutes. Now, I need to know if those choices are going to be a problem? I don't want to take my business elsewhere, but my friend Alice's cousin bakes and sells cakes out of her kitchen, so I do have other options," Rita continued to scowl pugnaciously at her niece while she directed her question to Melody.

"No, we can certainly bake all your choices," Melody replied calmly. "All your selections are just fine, and there is no finer cake baker than your niece here!"

Mollified, Kerry let go of her need to adjust Aunt Rita's cake menu, and smiled at her employer, "Awww shucks, boss-lady! You're the best!"

"Hmph," Rita grunted, clutching her giant purse more firmly to her chest, as if perhaps Melody and Kerry weren't to be trusted; she then adjusted her old-fashioned hat and exited with, "Okay then. I'll expect your delivery tomorrow afternoon, but no earlier than two pm, as I'll need an afternoon rest with all this working myself to death. And for what? Some ungrateful relatives who don't mind reaping the benefits of all my back-breaking labor!"

Kerry groaned, shaking her head. As soon as her aunt

was out of earshot, she commented, "Oh my God, Aunt Rita is something else, isn't she? No wonder Uncle Leroy left this earth... her sunny disposition probably poisoned him to death!"

Melody smiled, suspecting Kerry probably inherited her aunt's opinionated personality, and ability to talk at lightspeed. Though Kerry was liberally tempered with cheerfulness, Rita lacked pretty much any positive modifying trait.

Grab Strawberries and Sweet Lies for FREE with Kindle Unlimited or just o.99 to buy,

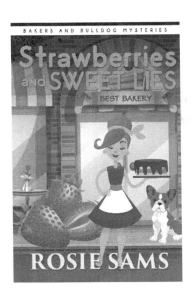

To be the first to find out when Rosie releases a new

book and to hear about other sweet romance authors join the exclusive SweetBookHub readers club here.

If you enjoyed this book Rosie would appreciate it if you left a review on Amazon or Goodreads.

This little bundle of Frenchie love would appreciate it too, this is Lila, also known as Piggy Pig.

Made in the USA
Middletown, DE
19 September 2022